Bluegrass Betrayal

by Robert Monahan

Lullabies
Lullaby Tiger Publishing

Bluegrass Betrayal

by Robert Monahan

Copyright ©2011 Robert Monahan

Lullaby Tiger Publishing
3969 Hillside Dr.
Lexington, Ky 40514

Tel: 859 327 8291
Email: Prowriter@robertmonahan.net
Web Page: www.robertmonahan.net

ISBN 978-0-9838036-4-5

Cover Design by Sharon Bradley
www.sharonbradleydesigns.com

Bluegrass Betrayal

by Robert Monahan

Physical struggles against the terrorist group, the Knights of the Caliphate, are not as painful as the emotional struggles with guilt, lust, and a search for redemption. In the midst of chaos and betrayal, some find peace and a second chance for love, while others find the dark side of their soul. All seek forgiveness, but who grants this merciful gift?

Bluegrass Betrayal is dedicated to my parents...

Kathleen Anderson Monahan (1919 - 1983
Francis James Monahan (1917 - 1996)

How fortunate I am to have been mentored by these
two beautiful people. I only wish to be born again to
them in another life

Bluegrass Betrayal

Chapter 1

Kentucky April 2001

"So, tell me," asked Dr. Evan Thompson of Tucker Flannery. "Who's gonna win the Derby this year?"

Tuck stood patiently watching Doc Thompson as the thirty-nine-year-old veterinarian moved from stall to stall in Fairhaven Farm's broodmare barn. The dogwood trees were in full bloom, and rose bushes were beginning to blossom. With just days to go until the Kentucky Derby, the greatest two minutes in sports, Fairhaven's head man was in a picture-perfect mood, having just celebrated his 49th birthday.

"Tell ya what," said Tuck, opening the stall door as the doctor moved his ultrasound gear in and around the young mare. "There's a bunch of good horses this year. But I think you saw the winner right here."

"You mean in the Bluegrass?"

The Toyota Bluegrass Stakes, a prominent grade one stakes race many consider to be the most prestigious of all Kentucky Derby prep races, had been run two weeks earlier at Lexington's famous Keeneland Racetrack. With one week to go before the Kentucky Derby, Doc Thompson and Tuck, being true horsemen, were growing more excited with each closing hour.

"That Millennium Wind ran wire-to-wire, but there's a lot of good speed this year," said Tuck. "I think this is gonna be one of the best fields Churchill's ever seen."

"Well, one thing's for sure, my bet's going to be on a Kentucky horse," said Doc Thompson.

"Ha," said Tuck, his sandy hair blowing down around his eyes. "Yer not goin' out on a limb, now are ya, Doc?"

Most horsemen knew that the majority of the field of twenty-plus three-year-olds poised to qualify for the 127th Run For the Roses were some of the fastest horses ever produced in the state of Kentucky. And both men were proud to be associated with them.

"So, who're you picking? Or don't YOU want to go out on a limb?" smiled Doc Thompson.

"Too early to tell," said Tuck. "But I wouldn't count ole Baffert out. He's got two contenders this year. That Point Given's just too big and bad, if you ask me."

"Yeah, but did you see the way Millennium Wind ran the Bluegrass?"

"You know what they say about the Bluegrass, Doc. If you want to win the Derby, don't win the Bluegrass."

"That's just an old barn tale," said the doctor. "You don't really believe that, do ya?"

"When's the last time a Bluegrass winner won the Derby?" chuckled Tuck.

"Well I know Northern Dancer won it. And look what he's done for the breed. Every other Thoroughbred in the game can be traced back to him."

"Yeah, but that's back before I was even in high school. Hey, Doc," said Tuck, stomping his feet, "you ever see so many of these caterpillars? They're everywhere this year. I'll bet half the trees on the farm are swarming with the dang things."

"Yeah, I know. I can't remember so many in one year."

"I walked out to my truck a while ago," said Tuck "and

a breeze blew up and it felt like it was raining caterpillars."

"Are you spraying for them?"

"Naw, don't want to do that. Never know how that might affect the animals. We're trying to burn 'em out, but we're not having much luck. Nobody's got the time, with all these mares in foal," said Tuck.

"Too bad you're not in the business of birthing caterpillars."

"Ain't that the truth?"

Doc Thompson smiled as he made his way over toward Sugar Berry, Fairhaven's twelve-year-old mare, bred a few months earlier. Mares are examined several times in their gestation period to determine the well being and sex of the offspring, allowing the farm to forecast its yearling sales more accurately.

"Well, let's see now, old girl, how're you doing today," said the doctor, preparing to scope the nervous mare. His smile changed to a frown, as he glanced at Tuck in alarm.

"What is it?" asked Tuck.

"No heartbeat, can't hear the foal."

Tuck stood 73 inches straight up and moved toward the mare's head, stroking the nose of the huge brown Thoroughbred.

"Nope, no heartbeat, this mare's carrying a dead foal."

"Doc, are ya sure? Couldn't it be masked or something'?"

"Easy, girl, easy," the doctor said soothingly, as he prepared to inspect the mare by hand. Placing the shoulder-length rubber glove on his right arm, he placed the rectal ultrasound into the mare's vagina, as Tuck steadied the horse from the opposite end.

"Nope. No good, Tuck."

With hardly a word spoken between the two horsemen, Doc Thompson continued scoping the rest of the Fairhaven mares until he reached Lishtie, a five-year-old gray, stabled a few stalls over from Sugar Berry.

"I don't believe this, Tuck."

"What?"

"You've got another one. I've never seen this. That's two in one barn in one day. I don't think I've ever even heard of this. I know I didn't find more than five all last year."

"No way, you've got to have a bad scope."

"That's what I'd have thought if it hadn't worked correctly on the first couple I monitored, but you've got another dead foal, look here," as he and Tuck verified the silence of the trans-abdominal ultrasound.

"I'll run some further tests at the lab, Tuck, but I know these foals are dead."

"Hell, Doc, that's two out of eleven, and yer not even through."

Tuck could feel the sweat breaking out on his forehead as Doc Thompson pulled out his cell phone and dialed the Kentucky Equine Research Center.

"This is Dr. Thompson; is Dr. Pehlagrem there?"

After several long and arduous moments, a warm, matronly voice came over the phone. "This is Dr. Pehlagrem."

"Dr. Pehlagrem, this is Evan Thompson. I'm over at Fairhaven Farm, and you're not gonna believe what's just happened."

Tucker Flannery couldn't believe it either. In all the years since Audra Blevins had hired him to manage Fairhaven Farm, he'd never experienced anything like two dead foals in one barn in the same day. Not, at least, since 1996, when several of Central Kentucky's foals were stillborn. But that was different; those foals had come through an entire eleven-month gestation period and had appeared to be healthy right up until their birth. The two found this morning were dead within the first three months of gestation. He'd never heard of that.

But Tuck wasn't a man who waited for the opportunity

to knock on his door; he was a man of action. He knew something had to be done, a quality he'd inherited from his mother, Ethel Flannery. She was a rough-and-tumble horsewoman from the day she broke her first mount to the day she gasped her last breath.

Tuck had to learn to deal with sadness from a very early age. He'd lost his only sibling, an older brother named Peter, in a car accident the evening of Peter's senior prom. Shortly after that, Tuck had to endure the painful passing of his mother. Raised by his father and taught the ins and outs of the equine business, he was hired by Audra Blevins to manage Fairhaven Farm when he was only twenty-two. But his fate had not completely turned for the better. On the July fourth weekend of that same year, he had to drive 80 miles to a lake-side town to claim the body of his father. A boating accident had taken the life of Tuck's last family member. Since then, he'd remained steadfastly dedicated and loyal to the farm. His family had taught him a love for horses, and that love was his remaining connection to them.

As Dr. Thompson finished examining the other mares, Tuck's mind raced ahead in preparation for what was to come next.

"Well, Tuck, I'm real sorry about this."

"Not your fault, Doc. Guess I better make a few phone calls." Opening his cell phone, Tuck dialed Audra Blevins' private number.

"Hello, Tucker, how're things today?" asked the sharp-minded owner of Fairhaven Farm.

"Mrs. Blevins, I've got some bad news."

"Oh?" She could tell by Tuck's voice that something was very wrong.

Chapter 2

Keeneland Pavilion - Lexington, Kentucky

The lights of the auction arena dimmed ever so slightly, creating a warm, cozy atmosphere as the echo of the auctioneer's gavel closed the sale at $210,000.00 of hip number 36, a dark gray filly.

"And now, ladies and gentlemen," bellowed Keeneland's head auctioneer, "hip number 37 from Stonecrest Farm, a bay filly out of Logician."

Directly across from the microphones and trying to concentrate on the horse sale sat Sasha Prahstomank, a 42 year-old representative from the United Arab Emirates. He was known as Darkside due to the large, although faint, birthmark on the left side of his face. Interestingly enough, the mark accentuated his fine features rather than detracting from them, making him noticeable in any setting.

"What ahma bid for this beautiful filly?" barked the auctioneer, "a Biddle, a buddle, a bidda 25, a 25, a bidda."

Dressed impeccably in his black suit and starched white oxford shirt, Darkside allowed the memory of the woman he'd met years earlier to waltz through his mind. After a chance encounter with her the previous night at a cocktail party, he hadn't been able to stop thinking about her since.

"45, gimme 45, I need 45, gimme 45."

He couldn't believe he was so consumed by her, and was annoyed. The sounds of the arena and the auctioneer seemed to waft in the air. He'd met many women in his worldly travels, especially since the ruler of Karoumi, Sheikh Efram Al-

Farouad, had promoted him to his current position. His responsibilities as director of the Karoumi Equine Training Center had taken him on many a global jaunt where he'd met countless women from many walks of life. But none had affected him the way this woman had. One of his many responsibilities was to purchase the finest Thoroughbred horses money could buy, which he ordinarily found extremely compelling; but if he continued to be so inattentive, he was on the verge of losing a potential stakes winner.

Unable to keep his mind on the bidding, he excused himself to those seated near him and walked outside. Noticing Darkside's arrival, Sela, one of his trusted attendants assigned to accompany him on his travels, quickly moved toward him. Seeing the young man hastening to his side, Darkside smiled and shook his head slightly, indicating that everything was fine. Understanding immediately that he was not needed, Sela returned to where he'd been standing.

Darkside walked slowly around the arena, taking care to notice as much as he could about the horses within his sight. Some were dark, almost black. Some were gray, some bay, and some chalk white, but the chestnut colts and fillies were his favorite.

Karoumi's equine stable was beginning to amass the caliber of Thoroughbreds necessary to develop its own lineage to compete worldwide, and Darkside took enormous pride in its success. It wouldn't be long, he hoped, before a true Triple Crown competitor would emerge from within the ranks of Karoumi's bloodlines. Always a positive thinker, he knew that winners like Secretariat and Citation came along only once in a lifetime, and he was not about to kid himself into believing in magic. He felt that winners were born, not made, and he knew that winning was more a matter of breeding than training, which was why he was here.

I must focus on the horses, he reminded himself walking the path leading up to the gate. *I must not chase frivolous thoughts. I must not think about... her.*

Returning to his seat, his attention was finally captured by a huge bay filly entering the bidding circle. Hip number 41 out of Ladymire Farms's Dancing Star was one of the horses he'd wanted, and his heart raced as the bidding quickly moved past $50,000.00

"Ho! Ho!" yelled the assistants who, having been placed strategically in the gallery, relayed the bids back to the auctioneer. "55, 65, 75. I've got 85 and ninety-thousand, thank you, sir."

The price escalated quickly as Darkside waited. He didn't like to get involved in the lower bidding. It was a habit he'd picked up from his sheikh, the man he used to accompany on these buying trips, until Darkside had been given full responsibility for running Karoumi's stables.

He thought about the many times he and the sheikh came to this arena, and how he admired the man who provided him the direction he so longed for in his life. Sheikh Efram was the kindest man he'd ever known. Darkside had also loyally served Efram's younger brother, Prince Rajad, before his death, knowing full well that Rajad had ordered him to bring the genetic poison to Kentucky, and to leave no one alive after infecting the top stallions in the industry. Rajad was the first person to see him as something more than a ruffian when they became fast friends as teenagers. He felt guilty that he couldn't have changed Rajad's thinking, or that he alone had survived that awful time when so many of Kentucky's finest horses were killed. Rajad had been his loyal friend and had been the only person to come to his rescue from a life of hellish torture in that stinking prison in Istanbul. But that was years ago, and so much had happened since then.

Darkside gazed on the most beautiful creatures in Allah's kingdom, wondering how he'd been able to do what he did, bringing such devastation to the breed, while not getting caught. His conscience roared, begging him to disclose what he'd done, but to whom? He often wanted to confess his sins, but again, to whom?

"245, 245, I've got 245, that's $245,000.00. That's my bid for this beautiful filly."

Darkside, trying to regain his focus, raised his hand.

"Ho!" yelled the assistant.

"250, I've got 255," responded the auctioneer.

The bidding gained momentum as the other high rollers entered the game. Sitting directly across and on the front row was Brendon Flynn from Ireland, a fierce competitor, as was Yuri Yokohashi, Japan's top horseman. This was the first horse any of them had been interested in, and when Flynn raised his hand, the pace quickened and the atmosphere intensified.

"Thank you, sir. And now I've got 300, I've got 300, and now I've, thank you, sir. And now I've got 350. Thank you, sir, 400, and 450, and I've got 475. Alright, ladies and gentlemen, I've got, thank you, 500, one half a million dollars."

The bidding exploded above $5,000,000.00 before Darkside ceased. He never went above three million for any horse and was surprised to find himself going so high before pulling out. He knew he was not on a limitless budget and that his sheikh was more frugal than either of the other two horsemen.

Disappointed by his purchase of only two of the four horses he'd wanted that afternoon, he left the sale and went to his hotel room, intending to take a nap before going out for the evening. Instead, he lay in his bed with thoughts of days gone by. Yet no matter how hard he tried, he could not stop thinking about... her.

Chapter 3

A Cocktail Party in the Bluegrass

She was tall and elegant, but not slim, as her large breasts were the envy of most women, and she looked like royalty dressed in her black cocktail dress and black high heels. Her flaming red hair was pulled into a bun and her makeup was immaculate as she stepped from the backseat of her silver Cadillac. She walked up the steps and through the ornate doors of the Robard mansion.

"Why, Callie, you look stunning," said Ragena Robard, as Callie Collquit made her way into the limelight of the 'horsey-set' cocktail party.

"Why, thank you, Ragena. And my, doesn't your home look just precious."

"Now, Callie, It hasn't changed a bit since the last time you were here," responded Ragena, kissing her lightly on the cheek.

Callie was among some 30 guests invited to the Robard party and would not have come at all if it hadn't been for a certain gentleman she'd hoped would show up. It was getting close to Derby and time for the horse folk to roll out the red carpet. With the auction winding down and Keeneland's spring meet in full swing, the excitement in and around Lexington was at an all-time high.

"Blanton's and water," said Callie, as the servant took her drink order.

"Hello, Callie," said Dr. William Biggerstaff, a renowned veterinarian and friend of the Robards. "It's always good to see you."

"Hello, Bill. I haven't seen you since last Derby Eve."

"Now don't you go too far with that; I've a reputation to uphold," said Bill, as he smiled and sipped his champagne cocktail.

People in the horse industry all know that when it comes to parties, Callie Collquit's annual Derby Eve gathering rates among the best; but most are unwilling to talk about what goes on. No one, however, turns down an invitation.

Held the night before the race, only those close to the ex-madam are given that special key which unlocks the door leading to her infamous basement and the real party. It's rumored that the devil himself would be in attendance if invited. One usually finds that most of the folks downstairs have shed their clothes and sprayed their bodies with special imported, fragrant oils. After several hits from a huge crystal bowl of pure cocaine, these lucky individuals are entertained by a band of hand-picked musicians who play blindfolded so as not to be able to reveal the depth of debauchery before them. It is sinful, to say the least, but no one ever complains, and in Callie's own words, "I separate the men from the boys, the girls from the toys, and the devil from the deep blue sea." The only thing out-of-sorts lately, and much to the surprise of the equine community, was the fact that, for reasons she would not disclose, Callie had decided not to hold her annual event, but to postpone the gala activity until the following year.

"You know my motto, Bill. See no evil have no life."

"Now, now," said Bill, not wanting to continue discussing her philosophy, especially with his wife within earshot.

Bill and Ilene Biggerstaff had met Callie several years before, when she was married to Herman Collquit, a wealthy coal operator who'd made it big during the boom years of the fifties.

Following the death of his first wife of 32 years, Herman and Callie had married in 1989, after a whirlwind courtship that left the high-society of the Bluegrass in stunned disbelief.

Most of them thought Herman an old fool for having thrown his life away after such a frivolous gold-digger as Callie, especially with the memory so fresh of his deceased, wealthy wife, Eleanor Playforth, whose blue-blood name had been the wind under Herman's wings for so very long. But Bill wanted to party and live the good life one more time before he died, and who could facilitate him in his endeavor more gainfully than Callie?

It was difficult at first, Callie having to play the good wife role to a powerful, over-achieving businessman. But she was a quick study and threw herself into running the farm as well as her role as hostess during the many parties the two would throw. Callie brought an element of style to Herman's life, which resonated enthusiastically with him. He loved her dearly and expressed it with his tenderness and affection, always treating her like a lady. There was no question that she was the queen of his heart, as well as his home, and he never missed an opportunity to let her know. It wasn't long before she found herself surprisingly happy and very much in love with Herman Collquit, a feeling she'd never thought she'd experience.

Unfortunately, as loving as Herman's heart was, it was physically weak. With the daily rigors of running a horse farm and an overactive sex life, it just couldn't take the pace. With his quest for tripping the light fantastic, the once destitute coal miner succumbed to a massive coronary at the golden age of 64.

Callie managed to survive the sad affair by rigorously maintaining the management of her 32 room mansion and 1,500 acre farm. Loyal to Herman's memory, she started a scholarship fund in his name, which provided an education to a deserving high-school graduate from the East Kentucky coal fields. She also remained involved with the social scene and was a valued part of the community, pledging her time and support to several of the local charities in the area.

Many of Lexington's former debutantes did not like Callie and held their noses high when she came within range.

Somehow, she always managed to keep the cauldrons of curiosity burning, affording her access to most of the important inner-circle gatherings. She was courted by several of the available men in the area, but most of the interesting ones she found were already married, which, of course, was out of the question. She may have had a sordid past, but she had promised herself that with her late-in-life respectability, she was going to remain a lady no matter the cost. She'd been loyal to her marriage and was determined to remain loyal to herself, but the nights seemed to grow longer and she wasn't getting any younger. She yearned for a companion.

The evening progressed as usual with the guests arriving between seven and eight, each with a story to tell or a question to be answered. Callie, with her lioness senses, kept her distance from most of the men as several pairs of female eyes flung daggers in her direction.

There was something special about Callie. Beneath the makeup and the years of hard knocks, she was a very cautiously calculating lady, neither vicious nor treacherous, and although she'd never admit it, she had a heart of pure gold hidden in her impressive chest. Some folks had more money, some were better looking, and some had even had more lovers, but there were few people in the world who were much smarter than Callie. She'd had to be, after the adolescence she'd endured.

A ward of the state at 11 and pregnant by 15, she was allowed to have the baby, but the infant girl was taken from her arms and placed for adoption. At 17, she was on the street turning tricks until she'd earned enough to buy a proper wardrobe and a car. With little money to spare, she took her brand of entertainment to Pauline's, a famous whorehouse in western Kentucky. So with all the things that Callie was or wasn't, she found herself, at 45 years young, to be in search of something that would bring meaning to her life. Something with an edge, she thought, as she stood alone near the large grand piano in the magnificent ballroom.

Sensing the penetrating stare of someone in the room, she turned slowly. Her heart jumped as the tall, attractive Middle Eastern man she'd met years ago and had bumped into the previous night, came into view. He was still as handsome as she'd remembered him with manicured hair, dark, flashing eyes, and a slightly noticeable star-shaped birth-mark on his face. Dressed impeccably in his jet-black tux, his striking stature did not fail to impress the red-haired beauty.

Who knows what causes sparks to fly between two people, but it was clear that from the moment they'd met in 1996, they'd burned brightly for each other. The heat had come rushing back when they had a chance encounter the previous night.

"Good evening, madam."

"Well, I declare," said Callie, almost blushing, which was quite unlike her. "How are you?"

"I am quite fine now. I had so hoped to see you this evening," said Darkside, bowing and kissing her hand. A man of few words, he could be very direct when he knew what he wanted.

"Oh, my," said Callie. "You are ever the gentleman, aren't you?"

With her vast experience in men, she was amazed at just how affected she was by this foreigner's demeanor.

"May I obtain for you a cocktail, madam?"

"Sure, what are you drinking?"

"I usually do not drink, but I will be happy to get something for you."

"How about a couple of bourbons have you ever had Blanton's and water?"

"No, madam, it is against my religion."

"Now wait just a minute. If you're gonna call me madam all night, I'm gonna leave right now. Please," she smiled, "call me Callie."

"Yes, mad..., Callie. A Blanton's and water, so it will be."

Chapter 4

They talked while Callie sipped her drink an hour or so before deciding to stroll outside in the crisp April evening. They looked almost heavenly as the glow of the white spring moon cascaded softly around them, painting them in a sweet, sensual manner. Standing close to his side as they gazed out into the pin-oak lined pasture, she allowed her head to rest on his shoulder with the tenderness of a butterfly. Feeling almost as lighthearted as when he'd been freed from prison, Darkside finally asked, "May I kiss you?"

Turning to face him and before she could respond, he'd placed his lips against hers and pulled her body into his.

It was nearing midnight when Colonel Robard asked his wife what had happened to Callie and her Arabian friend.

"Why, I don't know. Come to think of it, I haven't seen them all evening. They didn't say good night to me. Did they say anything to you?"

"Not a word. They did seem to get along well, don't you think?"

"Yes, and I wonder if that's why she isn't hosting her party this year. You don't think she's...?"

"She's what?"

"Oh, I don't know, but I'll tell you what... that Jenny Richardson sure has gained the weight. Did you see how much she ate? I didn't think we'd had enough shrimp for just her, let alone the other guests."

Darkside and Callie walked around the stallion barn at the Robard farm before deciding to sneak away to her home. Once there, she handed him a bottle of Dom Perignon to open before excusing herself.

He wandered about the ornate first-floor sitting room.

Seeing the picture of Herman Collquit on the inlaid mahogany table, he lifted the book-like gold frame holding Herman's picture and read the poem framed on the opposing side.

The Coal Miner

He spent his life down in the ground
But never knew the wealth.
He staked his future day by day
Until it claimed his health.

He warmed the world with winter light
Though his was dark and cold.
He spent his days in constant night
Pursuing nature's gold.

His dreams he gave to others
As they burned his weary soul.
His job, the miner's bleak reward,
A precious need for coal.

Heaven will repay him
For the efforts he so gave.
My humble prayer, his labour there
Did not produce his grave.

Callie changed from her black ensemble into a sheer, white negligé and white backless heels, before presenting herself to her olive-skinned suitor.

"Hello," she breathed, startling Darkside.

When he looked at her, his senses began to overload as she appeared like a vision from heaven or hell. He didn't know, nor did he care. Standing in front of him in all her delicious near-nakedness, her long silky hair falling around her shoulders, she leaned seductively against the doorway and gave him a broad but wicked smile.

"See anything you like?" she asked.

Still unable to speak, Darkside put down the picture and moved toward her. Gathering her slowly in his arms, he allowed his lips to cover hers tenderly at first. Then pressing harder, his tongue explored the inside of her mouth, finding hers waiting and willing. He slowly began kissing her neck while his hands moved over her magnificently silken skin.

"Ohhhhh," she moaned, as he positioned himself lower and lower, running his tongue in and around her navel.

"Oh pleeese, please," she breathed, bending her knees and lowering her body to a crouch.

They made love several times that night and welcomed the morning sun with faces of quiet satisfaction and an empty bottle of champagne. With her experience and looks, Callie could have her way with just about any man she chose. And now she chose Darkside, tempting and coaxing him into abandoning his Islamic lifestyle. By the end of the weekend, she had him hooked on her body and erotic ways, embellished by her endless supply of cocaine. They remained locked in blissful harmony for two days and nights before she asked him if he would consider accompanying her on a week-long trip.

"How long has it been since you've had a really nice vacation?" she asked.

"I have never had what you call a vacation. My life does not allow for such things."

"Then, baby, don't you think it's time you lived a little?

Have you ever been aboard a ship at sea where you are catered to around the clock. Where the only decision you make all day is what to wear for dinner? Where the food is divine and you can eat and drink till your heart's content. Have you ever done anything like that?"

Darkside did not know how to react. He wasn't sure if this was love, not so soon anyway. But what he did know was that he'd never felt this way about a woman before. When they weren't together, he could think of nothing but her. When they were together, she held him spellbound. Thoughts of the horses, Karoumi, and the sheikh were hardly a concern. While he was with Callie, she captivated him.

"I do not know if I could do that. I have responsibilities."

"Oh, to hell with responsibility... just live a little. Don't you deserve to live a little?" she interrupted.

"But I have my horses and my..."

"Are you the only one who can handle the horses? Don't you have any help? Of course you do. They can handle the horses. Hell, I'm only talking about a week."

Darkside's mind went into high gear pondering the thought of spending a week at sea with Callie. For several moments he sat motionless, deciphering all the things that had to be done.

"When would we leave?" he asked finally.

"Tomorrow. We could fly to San Juan and be out to sea by tomorrow night."

"We can do this so quickly? We do not need a reservation?"

"Honey, it's not what you have; it's who you know."

"I would have to make some phone calls."

"Baby, you don't have to call anyone. Your staff is smart and can handle one week. They'll know what to do, trust me."

Somehow her words brought an enormous feeling of relief as he felt the burden of guilt ascend from his shoulders. He was experiencing feelings he'd never known, and he liked it. With Callie, he felt safe, as though he could let down his guard. He felt that she would not only protect him, but complete him. He didn't know that she was a true temptress and could hold a man under her spell without conscience until she was ready to release him.

She was a prostitute of the highest calibre and enjoyed fleecing the men she'd serviced, powerful men who deserved what they got from her. And most of them loved whatever she gave or took from them. But Darkside was different; he didn't want anything from her, just her company. He was not egocentric, selfish, or vain, and she knew she didn't fully understand him. All she knew was that whatever he was, she wanted to be part of it. She wanted him. She also wanted the one-hundred-thousand dollars she'd been paid to take him on this cruise.

On that early April morning, just before the Bluegrass began its day, the two lovers boarded Delta's flight 1162 to Atlanta, en route to San Juan and the Caribbean.

Across the tarmac, outside a large hanger, Merrantz, International Inc., specialists in equine air transportation, prepared to ship the yearlings Darkside had purchased to Karoumi.

The Boeing 727's loading ramp had been lowered to the ground so the horses could board the plane. Flying stalls were built around each horse from the padded aluminum flooring up, with two aluminum bars on each side forming the walls and a bar across the back. The stall was partially assembled before the horse was walked into the plane and completed after the animal was settled in place. Two aluminum bars were attached to the rear of each of the sides, forming a three-sided stall.

The pilots walked up the portable stairway attached to the side of the plane, passing by Sela, who stood overseeing the loading process.

"We all here?"

"We are all here," nodded Sela.

"Where's the boss?"

"He will not be returning with us."

"Okay, whenever you're ready. Just give me the go-ahead, and we'll be on our way."

It was a smooth, uneventful ride across the Atlantic with a fueling stop in London. The plane entered Arabian airspace as the grooms and horse attendants scurried to find their seat belts in anticipation of landing at Karoumi's small airport. Noticeable was an empty seat, which was usually occupied by a man who had always accompanied the horses on the plane, a tall, dark, handsome man with a large birthmark on the left side of his face.

Chapter 5

Karoumi, in the United Arab Emirates

Sheikh Efram Al-Farouad, having spent the entire morning in a meeting with members of Karoumi's Municipal Counsel, opened the door of his inner office and walked pensively toward his secretary.

"Najema, do I detect that you are somewhere else today?" asked the sheikh lovingly.

"Oh, I am so sorry, sir, I was just," said the distracted 41-year-old spinster.

"I know what you are doing. You are thinking of that handsome man I have been seeing you with."

Najema smiled and said nothing.

"Will you be seeing him tonight? Or," Efram did not complete the question, not wanting to cause Najema any further embarrassment.

"I, ah yes, I guess so."

"I am happy for you, my dear. He seems to really like you. And you him, ah?"

She smiled and bowed her head as she blushed.

"And what is his name?" asked the sheikh.

"Abhur Sulari, but I call him Ab," she said, squirming in her chair.

It was true that Najema had never been married, nor had she ever been courted by any of the local gentlemen, but lately she'd been seen in the company of a stranger, a stranger who'd swept the unattractive, pudgy woman off her feet.

"I hope he brings you the happiness you so deserve," said

Efram in a fatherly tone.

Like most of Karoumi's citizens, Najema was completely devoted to her sheikh, having been his personal secretary since just before his father died nearly five years earlier. She was present when Efram met and married his true love Mella, helping him organize the wedding festivities and was, from that day forward, considered a dear friend and part of the royal family. The avuncular feelings Efram held toward Najema made him apprehensive about the stranger she'd been seeing. Efram knew that asking her questions regarding her private life would only make her uncomfortable, even though he himself was not at all comfortable about the man whom no one seemed to know.

Whatever it was, there was something he did not like about the stocky, dark-haired man with the evil eyes. Whether it was the way he carried himself, or the way he always seemed to appear from out of nowhere, never looking directly into one's eyes, Efram felt there was something wrong with this stranger, something he didn't trust. He knew Najema was smitten with him and that his attention to her was something the middle-aged woman needed, but Efram did not want to see her get hurt. His conscience told him that he should not meddle in business that was not his, no matter the cost. It was his sixth-sense regarding affairs of state, world-wide politics, and dealings with his younger brother Rajad that taught him to trust a certain feeling in his stomach when things were out of balance. He'd experienced the same feeling the first time he'd seen the stranger.

With no immediate family, Najema lived alone in one of Karoumi's newly designed apartments. It was true she was involved with a stranger, something she'd never before done in her life. Not that she'd ever thought much about it, but she did enjoy the attention this new man had lavished upon her. He'd been the first one to ever send her flowers, and that feeling alone had been one of the most enjoyable experiences of her life. She didn't question why, out of the blue, he'd wanted her and it didn't matter. She just remembered how he'd bumped into her that day in the park. He bowed and introduced himself, asking her name and if he could walk with her a while. Why he did it was not important to her. What was important was that he'd visited her every night for the past two months and had brought her gifts and had held her in his arms. She was falling in love, and that was all that mattered. She knew that she could easily find ways and reasons why this wasn't right, but that's not what she wanted. She wanted him, and that's all she allowed herself to think. Najema did admit that it seemed strange that her suitor asked so many questions about her work day and that of the sheikh's.

"The man with the birthmark on his face," he asked one day, when they first began their courtship. "What is his name?"

"Oh, that is Sasha."

"Does he always accompany the sheikh?"

"He is in charge of the stables. He usually accompanies the sheikh whenever he travels abroad. But the sheikh does not travel so much anymore."

"Why is that?"

"I do not know. I believe that Sasha does most of the travelling alone, since he is in charge of the horses. The sheikh must devote most of his time to the affairs of state. He is not really involved in the horses as much as before."

"Before?"

"Since Sasha has taken over the running of the stables. He is the one who does most of the travelling."

"I see," said Ab. "I see."

Chapter 6

Istanbul

The springtime breezes gusted unevenly, blowing the scents of the ancient city through the hilly, cobble-stoned streets, tantalizing nostrils with fragrances of fresh-baked bread and the early morning catch of the fishermen's nets. Since 658 BC, Istanbul has carried the label of "Queen of Cities" after its establishment by Greek colonists who named it Byzantium in honor of its founder Byzantas.

Known initially as "New Rome," Constantinople became the capital of the eastern segment of the Roman Empire in 330 AD, and remained for eleven centuries one of the most important political, religious, and cultural centers of Anatolia. Conquered in 1204, by the soldiers of the Fourth Crusade, the city resisted the campaigns of the Turkish tribes until it fell into the hands of the Ottoman Turks in 1453, led by Sultan Mehmed II who renamed the city, Istanbul.

The revolution of Hellenes against the Ottoman Empire in 1821, remains one of the most terrible events in Middle Eastern history, as the Orthodox churches within the city were set ablaze, while their leader Patriarch Gregorios V was murdered and hung at the gate of the Patriarchate in Fanari. As a continuing symbol of mourning, the gate has remained closed to this day. Following the First World War and the signing of the Peace Treaty of Moudros, the Ottoman Empire was divided between the Allies of the Entente into spheres of influence, as Istanbul came under international control.

In a hidden, out-of-the-way apartment atop one of the city's mid-town residential areas, a group of Turkish terrorists, known since the 1930's as the Knights of the Caliphate, gathered to discuss the final preparations of their current dark plan.

"I am to understand that he will soon be out of the way and that we can move without fear," said Tobarek Kazeem, leader of the Knights.

"Why not now, we could hit them before they even know what happened," said one of his cohorts.

"Patience, my friend, what is your hurry? You will have the rest of your life to spend your money, all ten million of it."

"Ten million dollars?"

"That is my price for their treachery."

Kazeem and the Knights of the Caliphate had been hired by Efram's younger brother Rajad, several years earlier, to plant a bomb on Trans Atlantic's Flight 718 from New York's Kennedy Airport bound for Rome. Had the bomb exploded, it would have killed everyone on board including Efram, affording Rajad not only the absence of his hated, over-protecting brother, but the right to succeed their father to the throne. Lucky for those passengers, that the bomb had been mistakenly removed from the plane allowing Efram safe passage on his return trip to Karoumi. Rajad, thinking that the bomb had failed to explode, didn't pay Kazeem and his Knights. But in the terrorist's mind, Rajad did owe the Knights an enormous sum, and Kazeem was determined to make them pay for the disrespect.

"But the prince is dead. This, this sheikh is not our enemy."

"Everyone is our enemy," said Kazeem.

"Did you kill his brother?" asked Stavrok.

"I only wish I had killed him. He deserved that and more."

Kazeem didn't know it was Jules Werhner who'd caused the untimely death of Prince Rajad. It was a night in which Rajad, hoping to rekindle their affair after having slapped her in a moment of rage, had invited her to dine with him at the royal palace. Having accepted his invitation, Jules appeared like a vision, dressed beautifully, but carrying a concealed substance she'd concocted earlier in her lab, a jelly-like poison she'd rubbed along the inside of his wine glass, which robbed the young prince of his life, killing him slowly, in an excruciatingly painful manner.

"Will they pay ten-million dollars?" asked Stavrok.

"Of course, they will pay. What can they do? He is the leader of their country, their rich country. You have seen how they live, their new schools, their new hospitals, all their horses. They have paid millions for just one horse, so ten-million to them is like ten dollars to you or me."

"How do you know how much they have paid for their horses?" asked Ramone, another of Kazeem's compatriots.

"Do not worry about how I know. I just know. If you would learn to listen more and talk less, then you would know these things."

"Ha, he thinks he knows. It is Sela. He is the one who knows," said Ramone, mockingly.

"How do we collect the money?"

"They will deliver it to us. How they do it is their problem," said Kazeem, hatefully.

It's hard for the Western mind to fully understand terrorism and the thinking behind its actions. It is unfathomable why these people believe that perpetrating cowardly acts of violence and treachery upon their fellowman will stand them well in the eyes of Allah. But such thinking remains the case in certain parts of the world, and Turkey is no different.

The Knights of The Caliphate got their unholy start only two years after the death of Turkey's first modern leader and father of the country, Kemal Mustafa Ataturk. What Ataturk was able to achieve during his short time in power was, nothing shy of phenomenal. He led a nation from the backward state of Mongol barbarianism into the modern age of the twentieth century.

Ataturk changed the calendar from Islamic to Western as well as the alphabet from the Arabic script, which had been used for more than a thousand years, to the Latin alphabet. And he abolished the age-old Caliphate, a traditional form of government which began after the death of Mohammed. That's where the Knights of the Caliphate got their start. They believed that the Caliphate was intended to carry on the legacy of Mohammed's authority, and that politically powerful Islamic entities, throughout history, including the Ottoman Empire, were incarnations of the Caliphate.

Unable to understand nor willing to accept that the average Turkish citizen was quite happy with Ataturk's accomplishments, the band of unscrupulous reprobates descended beneath its original charter to become nothing more than soldiers of fortune, who could be bought to perform any demonic deed at almost any price.

As the late afternoon clouds billowed lazily over the Persian Gulf, Kazeem sat motionless, planning his latest adventure.

Chapter 7

San Juan, Puerto Rico

The Matriarch of the Seas, an 80,000 ton ocean-liner, stood majestically awaiting her newest arrivals. Her massive hull kissed the mooring bushings holding her firmly within her birthing dock at Puerto Rico's most prestigious port-of-call. It was just past noon as Callie and Darkside, slightly drunk from all the cocktails they'd shared aboard the airplane, made their way jovially up the gangway and aboard the mighty vessel.

Clearing the electronic surveillance system, having been given the card-keys to their stateroom, they unpacked their clothes and strolled up to the ship's welcoming buffet luncheon on the eleventh deck. Before their eyes, lay an endless array of delicacies, including fresh strawberries, juicy melons of all kinds, seafood stews, steaming pasta, and fresh, local vegetables. There were breads hot from the oven, an endless assortment of desserts along another wall, and, of course, anything one could think of to drink.

"This seems almost sinful," said Darkside, following Callie through the buffet line.

"Isn't it wonderful? And honey, this is only the start."

They finished their meal and strolled about the outer deck near the top of the ship, holding hands and talking about what lay ahead in the upcoming week. Finding a quiet place behind a bulkhead near the rear of the boat, they stood watching the activity as vacationers continued to board the Matriarch several decks below. Moving toward the corner of the stern and looking over the railing, Darkside remarked how easy it would be to simply jump straight down into the water. Feeling uneasy at just how low the railing seemed to be, he noted that a tall person with a high center of gravity could easily be pushed off the boat from this vantage point.

"Out to sea and especially at night, he would never be found."

"Oh, that hardly ever happens," teased Callie.

"Well, if you wanted to lose someone, here is where you could do it."

"Is that all you can think about?"

Pulling her into his arms, the tall man with the birthmark on his face placed his lips over hers in a long, wet, passionate kiss. With the warm San Juan breeze blowing his hair about his face, he whispered gently in her ear, "I want you."

"How 'bout right here?" she asked playfully.

After several moments of kissing and groping, they made their way back to their cabin, locking themselves in serious passion until it was time to shower and dress for their first dinner at sea.

Her keel was laid the summer of 1990, in St. Nazaire, France, and her four French Peilstick diesel engines could carry 3,000 passengers and a crew of 850. The Matriarch of the Seas could make 24 knots through the Southern Caribbean, developing more than 30,000 horsepower at full speed.

When guests arrived that afternoon, she stood queen-like in every way with her white paint gleaming in the bright southern sun, and her flags at full mast. The darkness of night now veiled the city as her docking crew scurried about her massive forecastle like elves at Christmas, preparing her for a ten p.m. departure. The electrically driven propellers of the portside bow-thruster came alive, pushing the monstrous ship sideways out and away from port, as she announced her departure with a long, single blast from her harmonic air-horn.

Darkside and Callie stood in the open air by the railing along the top of the ship, transfixed with the serenity of the warm evening darkness and the twinkling of city lights surrounding them like a 360 degree theatre. Backing out from her birthing place, the Matriarch cruised out of the San Juan harbor, setting sail for St. Thomas, 92 nautical miles to the East.

"This is beautiful," said Darkside, his arm draped around Callie's shoulder.

She didn't respond but stood quietly breathing the warm night air, allowing the weight of her body to rest gently against his six-foot-one-inch frame.

Memories of vacations past began to overtake her thoughts, as she thought of her late husband and how often she'd tried to convince him to take a cruise, but to no avail. He'd had a fear of deep water, and no amount of pleading could convince him that being out in the middle of the ocean was safe. She thought of some of the other men with whom she'd cruised and how empty she'd always felt before, during, and after the ordeal. Usually bought and paid for, she carried no guilt about what she'd done or with whom, but this time things were different. This time she felt truly guilty, because the man she was with did not know that she was playing him. She'd manipulated him into accompanying her, and he didn't know that he'd been deceived. All she could do to rectify the situation was guarantee that he was about to have the best time of his life. That, she could deliver.

They remained on deck as the clear spread of the Milky Way became more visible the further they sailed from the lights of San Juan. They were making way at nine knots and would remain at that speed throughout the night, the ship creasing the still water with noticeable steadiness.

"Can you believe all those stars?" said Callie. "Did you know that there are more stars in the universe than all the grains of sand on all the beaches in the world?"

"No! Where did you hear that?"

"On one of those Nova shows. What's his name, the guy that died a few years ago. Carl, something, he said it."

"How would he know that?"

"I don't know, but he sure was a smart man. I do know that."

The events of the evening, including dancing, cocaine, and late-night sex, blended well into the morning as the sun peeked its brightness through the curtains of the stateroom porthole. Callie, waking before Darkside, sprang to the window realizing that they were not only docked in the Charlotte Amalie port of St. Thomas, but were moored directly next to the largest ship she'd ever seen, Disney World's beautiful Magic.

"Wow!" she exclaimed, as Darkside turned over, trying to shield his eyes from the blinding rays.

"What?"

"You should see this ship. It's huge. And it's painted black."

"Do I have to?" he groaned.

"Come on, babe. It's time for breakfast. Aren't cha hungry?"

"Hungry? We just ate."

Darkside maintained an almost perfectly trim figure, honed from years of eating just twice a day and only whole, unrefined, sugarless foods.

"Wanna skip breakfast and just get some coffee?"

"No, we can eat. I'll just have some fruit, but you, you should eat what you like. This is your vacation."

"This is OUR vacation," said Callie.

"I know. I just want you to be happy."

"Baby, I don't know when I've ever been happier."

"I thought I was in shape, but I'm not sure I can keep up with you."

Throwing themselves together in record time, they quickly gobbled a light breakfast of fruit, cheese, bagels and coffee before leaving the ship for a morning of shopping and strolling about the charming area of Charlotte Amalie. Taking Darkside through several of the local shops, Callie suggested he try on some colorful tropical shirts and shorts. She bought him a complete ensemble of vacation attire worthy of Arabian royalty.

With his new clothes and hand-made sandals, sporting a pair of gleaming Chevalier sunglasses, Darkside stood preening before a shop mirror like a Greek god, while Callie looked on approvingly.

"Oh yes, now you look like a royal prince."

Her remark reminded him of his loyalty to his sheikh, causing him to turn and look at her.

Without saying a word, he stood transfixed, thinking of how he was being missed so many miles away. How was his sheikh feeling about him?

"What's the matter, baby? Don't you like the way you look?" she asked.

"Not bad, not bad."

"Not bad? You look better than anyone on this ship. And that includes me."

"Oh, I do not believe that I look better than you. No one that I have seen looks better than you, madam."

"I think we look pretty damn good, you and me. Maybe I'll let you escort me to dinner tonight."

"As you wish, madam, as you wish."

Chapter 8

Lexington, Kentucky

Johnny Stone sat motionless as he held the phone to his ear in disbelief. In all his years covering the horses as a sports writer for the Lexington Herald Leader, he never imagined that something as terrible as stillborns and foals dying could be happening, not just once, but twice. It had been several years since the Central Kentucky area had been plagued by a plethora of stillborn foals, but the dreaded disease had been contained and the industry saved from what appeared to be a slow, painful demise. Until this phone call, he'd thought that whatever had caused the deaths of so many foals that year had disappeared.

"When?" asked the dismayed reporter.

"Last Saturday, two in one barn. We're receiving reports from several farms in the area. I'm about to send my entire staff out to the field," said Dr. Meredith Pehlagrem.

Replacing Dr. Frederick Radabaugh as Director of the Livestock Disease and Diagnostic Center at the University of Kentucky, Meredith Pehlagrem well remembered the stillborn problems five years earlier. Employed at the time in the Middle East by the Karoumi Equine Research Center and knowing Prince Rajad's lover, Jules Weherner personally, Meredith was on the verge of solving the infamous malady. Then Jules was killed, taking to her grave the only truth in the matter. Meredith was certain that Jules had been involved in the unfortunate fate of the Thoroughbreds but was unable to verify her information. Following her return to the states,

Meredith was offered a job at the Kentucky Equine Research Center by Dr. Radabaugh after she and her fiancé, an equine research specialist, had flown in to help solve the mysterious foal deaths.

"Oh, not again," said Johnny. "Is it the same thing as before?"

"That, I don't know. But, I'll tell you this. The only reason I'm calling you, Mr. Stone, is the way your paper handled this situation the last time we had a problem. Until we know something definite, I would really appreciate it if you wouldn't print anything."

"I'll do the best I can, Doctor, but I don't make those decisions. How long until we know something?"

"Well, at this time I really can't say. I'll call you as soon as I can provide a definite answer."

"Alright, but how long do you think that'll take?"

"I've had about six different reports, as we speak. But I don't know the extent of the problem. I don't know the exact locations, farms, and horses. Nor do I have any numbers. But I do know that fetuses are aborting early and that there have been about ten or 12 so far."

"Doctor, is it bad?"

She hesitated for a moment before answering. "It's bad."

Johnny allowed the sentence to hang in the air before responding, "Well, thanks, Doctor. I'll do the best I can."

Leaning back in his chair and remembering the incidents five years earlier, Johnny thought about how he was going to handle the story.

Should I tell the boss? He thought. *Why not? Hell, it's his problem too.* But he remembered how Sam Stroub had pushed him to write about the foal deaths before he'd wanted to, and after he'd promised the doctor from the equine center that he'd hold the story. *I sure as hell don't want to get into that mess again,* he thought.

He didn't have to wait long, as Sam, seeing Johnny in such a pensive position with his feet up on the desk and his eyes staring off into space, stopped by his office just in time to interrupt the silence of the moment.

"Gooooood mornin', and what in the world are you so intently thinking about? You're not planning your retirement ceremony again, are ya?" Sam always had a way of breaking into Johnny's office at just the wrong time.

"You are absolutely not going to believe who just called me," said Johnny, furrowing his brow into a serious mask.

"Who? No, don't tell me. It's that new defensive coach over at the university wanting your advice on how he's going to play eight men on the line of scrimmage."

"Very funny, get hold of yourself. You remember what happened five years ago?"

"Hell, I can hardly remember what happened five days ago, much less five years ago," said Sam, in his usual insensitive manner.

"The foals!"

With that, the joviality of the room seemed to evaporate, as Sam's expression went from a smile to a frown.

"What about the foals?"

"I just got off the phone with that doctor over at the research center. She told me that they've received reports of foals dying again. She doesn't know why, but she's gonna call me back. She doesn't want us to print anything until they're ready."

"Holy mother of God, alright, if what she says is true, this is your lead story. Drop everything else and focus on this. Damn! I can't believe it," said Sam.

"I'll a, I'll just, hell I'll just stay by the phone until she calls."

"Now look, they never found out what caused this the last time, did they?"

"Don't think so. They quarantined a bunch of horses, but I don't think they ever stated that they'd found a definitive cause."

"Damn," said Sam. "Well, keep me posted. Maybe we

should get out in the field ourselves."

"I don't know. She did us right the last time, and I don't want to stir up a hornet's nest unnecessarily."

Sam looked at Johnny for a long moment before turning and walking away. Johnny, remaining silent, just sat with his feet on his desk, staring at the wall.

Chapter 9

The Kentucky Equine Research Center

"Good morning, people," said Dr. Pehlagrem, attempting to bring the room full of scientists and doctors to order. It was almost ten o'clock and many of the folks Dr. Pehlagrem had brought together, some of the finest minds in the business, were consumed with the happenings of the day.

"As many of you already know, we are having another stillborn problem, or should I say an early fetus loss problem, and we do not have a solution, or even a known cause."

Dr. Roger Pulliam, having recently earned his doctorate from the University of Kentucky, immediately opened the forum. "Didn't we see this a few years ago?"

"We had a problem some years ago with several stillborn foals. That is correct."

"Is this the same problem, or do you see any differences?"

"We are seeing mares losing foals during early pregnancy, some by the 40 day check. This is not the same as what we experienced during the previous foal-death period. Most of the foals a few years ago had completed gestation. This is presenting quite differently."

"As I recall," said one of the doctors gathered in the room, "we didn't find a definite cure for the problems we had back then. Is that true?"

"Correct, we did not find the cure, but we were able to contain it."

Dr. Pehlagrem knew that the stillborn problems five years earlier may well have been due to sabotage, but since she had no proof nor could she substantiate such a claim, she thought it best to remain silent. But as she spoke, memories of overhearing Jules and Prince Rajad talking about a poison flashed through her mind.

"However, this time, I would like us all to take a more hands-on approach. We are receiving reports of foal deaths every day, and I think we need to get out to the farms as quickly as possible."

"What's been reported so far?" asked an equine epidemiologist.

"Foals born underweight which die within hours, redness in the eyes, some red-bag deliveries," said Dr. Pehlagrem.

A red-bag delivery is one in which the placenta either comes out ahead of the foal or covers the foal causing death due to a lack of oxygen.

"Are we keeping this under our hats, or are we seeking outside help?" asked one of the reproductive physiologists who'd remembered the instructions given by Dr. Radabaugh during the previous foal-death crisis.

"Good question. I've already called the Herald Leader and asked them not to print anything until we know what's going on. I don't think we should be disclosing information to anyone until we can collectively understand what we are up against."

Dr. Marion Tramlecki, a 60 year-old parasitology expert and the senior scientist in the room said, "We need to be looking at toxins. Mold in the grass, that kind of thing. We've had some pretty erratic weather this spring, and we've also had an over-abundance of tent worms."

"You mean those caterpillars in the fruit trees?" asked Roger.

"Yes, and they're everywhere. You know how toxic they can be."

"Alright, everyone has a cell-phone, correct?" asked Dr. Pehlagrem. "I'll be here at the center if you need me, so let's stay in touch, people, and plan to meet back here tomorrow morning at eight sharp."

She assigned each member of the team a list of farms to call on, some of which had reported problems, others which had not. They wanted to canvass as many farms as possible in the shortest period of time. Most of the farms were unaware their mares might be carrying dead foals, but, sadly enough for all concerned, they were about to find out.

Chapter 10

It was another hot day, the relentless sun scorching the white Arabian Desert as Efram, having finished his afternoon tea, asked Najema once more if she'd been able to contact Darkside.

"He has not responded to any of his messages."

"Did you try yesterday?" asked a concerned Efram, knowing full well that she had tried several times.

"Yes, and I left a message each time."

Efram was puzzled. It was the first time Darkside had failed to accompany the newly purchased horses, and it was unlike Karoumi's most loyal constituent to be so incommunicative, and for so long. It had been almost a week since he'd heard from Darkside, and he was truly worried.

"I hope he is not ill. Please call Doctor Hargrove in Kentucky. He may know of his whereabouts."

Najema began to retrieve Dr. Hargrove's phone number from her computer, as Efram said, "And if he does not answer, please call Colonel Robard or Mrs. Blevins. Do not stop calling until you reach someone. I will be waiting for your response."

Najema knew by the sound of the sheikh's voice that he was distraught. Because he was normally calm and collected, she'd never seen him so distressed, not, at least, since the time he'd found out about Mella's ordeals during her adolescence. That's when Najema had realized how unworldly and innocent Efram was. She did not think that any man, least of all one with the money, power, and position that Efram possessed, could have possibly been so naive.

However, it was a huge surprise to both Najema and Mella that the leader of a United Arab Emirates country would not have known about one of Arabia's centuries-old cultural rituals. The removal of the adolescent woman's clitoris was a barbarous custom instilled in ancient times to prevent unwed pregnancy and the desire for extra-marital activity. Of course women who had undergone this procedure were unlikely to enjoy sex with their husbands either. Efram, upon learning of this, ordered the practice outlawed with a promise that anyone caught performing the wretched act, especially any of Karoumi's doctors, would spend the rest of his or her life behind bars. Not normally a leader to dictate policy, Efram had reacted immediately after hearing of Mella's torturous ordeal. Without anesthesia, and with her mother and two of Mella's aunts holding her down, the local Shounktur, known for his mastery with a knife, carved the small element from within the 13 year-old's vagina, leaving her screaming in agony. It was more than Efram could take as he immediately called his Municipal Counsel together to order his decree.

"Your Highness," said one of his advisers in a stern but respectful voice, "this is a matter for our women to administer. It is their practice."

"Until now!" ordered Efram, with an angry look on his face. "Our women have endured this butchery long enough. This will not be a part of our culture. From this day forward, I forbid it."

The members of the Counsel sat dumbfounded. Never before had Efram, nor his father before him, been so adamant and decisive. There had always been room for debate, and it was usually encouraged, but this time it was different. Everyone in the room could see the fire in their leader's eyes as he talked about the penalty of prison and the absolute abolishment of the practice.

At first, some of the Council members were upset over the ruling. But, as time passed, the average citizen of Karoumi came to understand that their sheikh wanted only the best for them, regardless of traditional ties and ancient bondages. It was time to move ahead, and Efram was proving to be the perfect man for all seasons, allowing Karoumi to progress dynamically into the 21st century.

It was this ruling that brought Mella closer to him, creating the desire in both to expand their family. But natural childbirth was something the royal couple would have to learn to live without. An Ob/Gyn Efram had recruited to supervise Karoumi's Neonatal Unit had told the family that Mella's reproductive system had been damaged, possibly due to the over-taxing aspects of her clitoral removal, preventing her the ability to sustain a normal pregnancy. Although they tried every way imaginable at first, Mella could not conceive the child they both desired.

But in their third year, Mella found herself miraculously with child. Allah had heard and had answered her continuous prayers, but during a horrible, uncontrollable miscarriage, Mella, unconscious and anemic, bled to death in her royal bathroom after fainting sometime during the night. The sheikh, having suffered the loss of his mother, father, and brother, buried not only the last remnant of his immediate family, but his partner, his confidante, and the love of his life.

Following the burial, Efram drove himself to longer working hours for the benefit of his people. He cherished the work and found that it often kept sadness from his mind until the dark hours that found him alone in prayer or fitful sleep. He couldn't bear the thoughts of his child or the love of his life but could not forget them either. He lived in a cauldron of exhaustion and ill health. The only thing offering him peace was the training of Karoumi's horses and the man whom he'd promoted to master them.

Chapter 11

Approximately 70 kilometers north of Jask, a medium-sized community along the southern coast of Iran, in an out-of-the-way inlet, moored at a small, run-down, forgotten fishing port, rested the aging Galeos. She was a worn-out, rusty, retired oil tanker that had seen better days. Down in the hull of the once productive, ocean-weary vessel sat Tobarek Kazeem and the Knights of the Caliphate.

"We must sail slowly, as though we are on our last mission, like we are taking this ship to her final resting place. That way we will not attract attention. Does everyone know what he is supposed to do?" asked Kazeem, not expecting any questions after reviewing the plan constantly for the last several days.

It was a shame that a man with the mind of Kazeem would have chosen such an ignoble path. Had the proper example been set for him, or sufficient love shown to him, who knows what this man could have accomplished? But life so often deals from the deck unconscionably, without the least bit of care, allowing free-will to reign wholeheartedly over even the smallest smidgen of favoritism or fair play.

"Remember," said Kazeem, "they will not be alarmed with our presence, so do not act as though we are criminals. We are merely on a mission of revenge. We will all be blessed for our actions."

The sun was beginning to set as the ancient tanker disembarked from the tiny inlet. Flying the friendly flag of the United Arab Emirates, it made its way slowly and deliberately out into the Persian Gulf, northwest toward one of the newest ports in Arabia, the oil-rich Port of Karoumi.

Following an uneventful night crossing the Persian Gulf,

the Galeos made the Port-of-Karoumi early the following morning, as Kazeem and his cohorts brought the ship toward the docking platform.

Prior to their entry into the port, the Knights were met by a contingency of port authority members who approached the ship in a small police boat. Clambering up the portside ladder, the dock-master walked briskly toward Kazeem who had positioned himself inside the helm of the ship.

"What are you doing?" asked the dock-master.

"Allow me to introduce myself, I am Tobarek Kazeem and this is my crew. We have come here on a mission of mercy."

"What mission. I was not told of any mercy mission? You must leave this port at once."

"We will be most happy to leave, but we must first deliver our package to your country."

"What package?"

Without the slightest hint of anxiety and acting as though he were on a mission from Allah, Kazeem managed to convince the port authority to unload a large container from the cargo hold of the ship.

Kazeem's men docked the Galeos as well as could be expected, and went to work unloading a huge box onto the dock.

"What is it?" asked the dock-master.

"It is a gift for you. We have been asked by the United Nations to deliver this vehicle to your country and your hospital. That is all I know."

Un-boxing the crate, the men on the deck revealed a gleaming, white four-wheel drive vehicle with a large red cross painted on the side.

"We have been told nothing of the arrival of this gift," said the dock-master on duty that morning.

"You can ship it back, if you like. But I am to understand it is a present for your hospital. We have been asked to deliver it to you, and now we have delivered it. It now belongs to you."

"I am not sure we can take it," said the dock-master

rubbing his chin.

The unsightly oil tanker, having made a sorry statement by its dilapidated appearance, created a tone of distrust with the dock-master. Turning to face Kazeem, he was surprised when he found himself peering down the muzzle of a small Russian handgun.

"And now, my good friend, would you be so kind as to accompany me on board," ordered Kazeem, pointing to the gangway.

The two men disappeared, unnoticed, into the bowels of the ship where the dock-master was bound and gagged. Moments later, Kazeem and his gang returned to the vehicle, and the entire entourage left the dock en route to the royal palace.

Kazeem laughed loudly as the white vehicle roared toward the sheikh's royal palace with the map provided them by their local constituent; a man who, for the last several weeks, had been romancing the sheikh's secretary.

Chapter 12

They strolled into the huge dining room located on the fourth deck at exactly eight o'clock, Darkside in his black tux and Callie in her black, sequined gown. They looked like models who'd just stepped out of Vogue magazine as their head waiter, Frederick, held Callie's chair as she sat down. Seated at the table for six were Ginny and Sid Bishop from Omaha, celebrating their 25th wedding anniversary, and Sarah and Kyle Saveroy, newlyweds from Toronto.

After introductions and handshakes all around, the head waiter presented each guest with a menu of the evening's delicacies, while his assistant filled water glasses. They talked among themselves as Callie, with her outgoing personality, took the lead.

"My name's Callie, and this is Sasha," said the voluptuous red-head.

"Hi, we're the Bishops from Omaha; I'm Sid and this is my wife Ginny."

Sarah Saveroy also spoke up, introducing herself and her husband Kyle as the soup, salads, and appetizers were served.

"So," said Darkside to the Saveroys, "you are just married? Well, congratulations."

"Why, thank you. How long have you been married?"

"We are not married," he answered, glancing sideways at Callie.

"But that doesn't stop us, does it, honey?" said Callie with a wink.

"Well then," said Kyle, raising the glass of water in front of him. "Here's to us."

"To us," repeated Darkside.

"And to a safe and wonderful cruise," said Sid.

Starters for the evening meal included Mandarin and grapefruit cocktail with Grand Marnier liqueur, a smoked fish platter, and Gruyere cheese finished with sweet, red pepper Coulis. The soups were cream of tomato, chicken consommé, and chilled sugar pea. Salad was a seafood penne tossed with seared mussels, shrimp, diced tomatoes, and garlic, finished with fresh herbs. And the main entrées: royal fillet of cod, rosemary chicken, prime rib of beef, and vegetable brochette.

"Do I have to pick just one?" laughed Callie.

"No, madam, you may have whatever you prefer."

"Ah, well, I'll just have the prime rib. That should be enough for now, don't you think?"

"Oh yes, madam."

The dinner was exceptionally good, as they'd ordered a bottle of Chateau Lafite Merlot. They were enjoying their first sips of coffee when the waiter presented them with the dessert tray. Callie selected the almond chocolate cake, while Darkside ordered the low-fat, baked apple turnover with vanilla ice-cream.

"Now that's what I call dinner," said Callie, sipping the last remains of her third cup of coffee.

"But wait," said Sid, signaling the waiter carrying the shiny shot glasses in which the evening's liqueur was served. "It's not over yet. Six," said Sid, as the waiter approached the table.

"But tell me. What's tonight's choice?"

The tall, handsome waiter's face lit-up as he explained the home-made concoction prepared especially for toasting.

"Tonight we have what is called a chocolate kiss."

"Alright, kisses are good," said Sid. "Give us each a round."

The waiter placed a glass of the sweet liqueur in front of each guest, while Sid signed the receipt for the drinks.

"Okay, now here we go," lifting his glass toward the center of the table.

"And to us each a healthy life," said Callie, as she and Darkside held their glasses up to toast.

"Oh, that's good," said Sarah, as she drained her glass.

"God bless us all," echoed Kyle.

"Now what?" asked Darkside.

"Just follow me," said Callie.

Like two kids at recess, they quickly made their way up several flights of stairs to where the ship's photographer had set up shop in the center of the mezzanine near the glass elevators. A lady in a black evening gown played music from the Phantom of the Opera on the Baldwin grand piano, as water from the magnificent fountain shot upward from the backs of two large whales, cascading down into the stone-lined basin. Callie and Darkside stood hand-in-hand awaiting their turn to pose.

"That's it, now turn your heads and look up. That's good, that's good," said the photographer, as Callie stood with her back to Darkside.

"Now, face each other and look at me. Good. Now hold it, good. Okay, they should be available for your review tomorrow morning."

"Well," said Darkside, "that was easy."

Taking the elevator up to the eleventh deck, they strolled out under the stars as the moon laid a silvery path across the shimmering, warm water.

"Isn't this lovely?"

"You are lovely."

"And so are you," she said, sliding into his arms for a long, delicious kiss.

"Well then, let's just stay out here till the sun comes up?"

Chapter 13

"Karoumi Airport, this is Lear 427ZL9'r signaling emergency. Come in Karoumi."

"Lear 427ZL9'r this is Karoumi Airport, what is your emergency?"

"Yes, Karoumi, we have lost an engine, and are losing altitude rapidly. Do we have permission to land?"

"Permission is granted, what is your altitude?"

"We are at 6,000 feet, and have only one engine. Can you vector me to your nearest runway?"

"Please correct your heading to 127 degrees, and try and maintain altitude. I have you on my radar screen."

"Roger Karoumi. How far is it to your nearest runway?"

"You should see the lights in about six minutes."

"Roger Karoumi, we will maintain heading 127 until we see the lights."

Lear flight 427ZL9'r landed safely at the Karoumi Airport, and, following orders from the control tower, taxied toward the hangers at the far end of the runway. As the pilot stepped from the aircraft, he was met by one of the mechanics from the repair shop. Explaining in a thick Turkish accent that one of his engines had stopped running, he was met by a municipal guard who'd been called by the tower to investigate the incident.

"I do not know what went wrong. I only know that my engine stopped during the flight."

"What are you doing in Karoumi's airspace?" asked the guard.

"I am a student pilot. I must have gotten lost during flight. The weather was very bad and there was a lot of sand."

"Remain with your aircraft until our mechanics can look at

it."

"I understand. That is fine. Thank you for your hospitality."

The pilot walked inside the hanger as one of Karoumi's technicians approached.

"I won't be able to look at for another couple of hours. Just hang around here, and we'll get to it as soon as possible."

"I will remain here," said the pilot.

Meanwhile, Kazeem, and his cohorts had managed to sneak through the township of Beladesh without the slightest inkling of concern until their Jeep stopped just outside the walls of the royal palace. From the information they'd been supplied, they knew exactly how to enter the palace unnoticed. Once inside the building, they crept, stealthily along the main floor until they were confronted by one of the royal guards. Overpowering him noiselessly, they positioned themselves strategically outside the sheikh's office suite awaiting the signal from Kazeem to move in.

Efram had spent the morning pensively watching the newly arrived horses being walked about the stables of the equine center, normally a happy occasion. With heart-felt concern and worried about what might have befallen Darkside, he returned to his office. Pacing the floor, he was unable to eat his breakfast which had been prepared for him and placed on his desk.

"Najema," he called, "please try again."

But as Najema reached for the phone, she caught a glimpse of the man she'd been seeing each night for the last several weeks walking hurriedly through the open foyer just outside the office suite. Her heart jumped, but her mind quickly controlled her feelings. *What is he doing here at this time of the day?* She thought. *Has he come to surprise me?*

Uncharacteristically ignoring the sheikh's request, she bounded for the door in search of her lover. Failing to find him, she returned to her desk and placed the long distance call.

"Mrs. Robard, please."

When the voice of Mrs. Robard came on the line, she asked, "Mrs. Robard, would you please hold for the Sheikh of Karoumi?"

Picking up the phone in his office, the worried sheikh began, "Yes, Mrs. Robard, thank you. I am well, thank you. I am somewhat concerned that I have not heard from my Equine Director, Sasha? Have you seen him recently?"

"Why no," said the cheerful voice, 7,000 miles away. "He was here at a cocktail party the last I saw of him."

"How long ago has that been?"

"Well now, let's see. I think I had that party last Thursday night. Would you like me to try and locate him for you?"

"Would you, please."

"I'd be more than happy to."

"Thank you, Mrs. Robard. My secretary will tell you where I can be reached."

"Okay, then. I'll call just as soon as I know something."

Najema was in the middle of giving Mrs. Robard the phone numbers of the royal palace when the line went dead. Tapping the receiver several times, she was in a state of confusion when her boyfriend quietly entered the room, followed by Kazeem and his men dressed in black shirts and slacks, each brandishing a small snub-nosed pistol.

"Remain quiet, and you will not be hurt," whispered Ab.

One of the men removing a tiny syringe from a shoulder bag, walked over to Najema and injected her with 40 cc's of Staligyn, a powerful, fast-acting sedative.

"No, please," she whimpered, backing into the wall, her eyes wide with horror, but to no avail. As the drug began taking effect, three of the men rushed into the sheikh's inner office, overpowering him by administering a second syringe loaded with the sleep-inducing drug.

It was over quickly as Najema was dragged into the inner office and laid on the floor by the sheik's desk. The sheikh, his arms dangling at his sides, was manhandled out to the vehicle in which the kidnappers had arrived.

"Wha, whe you tak'n me?" asked Efram, hardly able to put a complete sentence together. "Do exactly as I say and you will not be hurt," said Kazeem in a stern voice.

While the cramped vehicle made its way to the airport Kazeem sent a beeper signal to one of his Knights waiting at the airport. A few moments later, Lear 427ZL9'r came alive as both its engines began to warm up. The escape vehicle, carrying the sheikh, Ab, Kazeem, and his accomplices, reached the airport and the awaiting jet within minutes, with no one noticing their arrival. They quickly boarded the plane and began taxiing out to the runway.

"Yes, Karoumi Center, this is Lear 427ZL9'r, performing a mechanical check," said the pilot. "I would like permission to take the runway."

"Go ahead, 427ZL9'r. You may take runway two left," answered the controller, unaware of what had transpired. The Lear jet, the terrorists, and the unconscious sheikh flew into the cool, thin air high above the Arabian Gulf.

Chapter 14

Their second day at sea found Darkside and Callie docked at Philipsburg, on the island of St. Martin in the Dutch West Indies, 114 nautical miles southwest of St. Thomas. After a morning of shopping and merriment, the vacationing lovers relaxed by the side of the ship's pool, both with an ice-cold, frozen Marguerita in their hands and a smile on their lips.

"Wanna little nose candy to go along with that?" asked Callie with a wry grin on her face.

They'd been using cocaine since their first night together in Lexington, and Darkside, for the first time in his life, was becoming attached, not only to the coke, but to Callie and her temptress ways.

"Not here?"

"Of course, not here," she said, her enormous breasts spilling over the top of her curvaceous, black bathing suit. She looked beautiful with the suntan oil lying deliciously on her perfectly bronzed skin.

Following their return to the room, she delicately doled out lines of cocaine on the mirror she'd brought for just such an occasion. Sniffing a thick white line into each nostril, Darkside lay back on the bed, awaiting the effects of the narcotic. Repeating the procedure herself, Callie asked, "What do ya think?"

"Very good."

"Very good hell, that's perfect, baby. Perfect."

While he lay on the bed, she began removing her bathing suit. First, she slid the shoulder straps slowly and seductively down each arm. Darkside, the effect of the cocaine kicking in, began to become aroused. Then, while looking back at him in a very seductive manner, she turned around and slowly inched the tight suit down past her buttocks, winking at him just as it fell to the floor.

With their bodies covered in oil, they made love with raucous abandon, as though there were no tomorrow, she on top, pinning him to the bed. Her body, like a slippery piston, moved violently up, down, and around, as though she were an integral part of an eccentric rotation device. She did it all by herself as the only thing he had to do was remain firm and erect, while holding on for dear life. Out of control, she brandished a distorted, fiendish look he'd not seen, somewhere between agony and ecstasy. Finishing the wild encounter, they lay in each other's arms until he found the strength to ask how she felt.

"Wonderful. Just, wonderful. You are the best lover I've ever known."

"And how many have you known?"

Turning to face him and hesitating before she spoke, she responded with a semi-serious look on her face.

"Now, let's not go there. Just say that I've had enough to know when I'm with a real man. And you are quite the man."

"I do not know about women. I have never lived with one, so I know very little of them. I spend most of my time with my horses."

"Well, you sure know how to please me. There's something about you I find irresistible. You have a quiet confidence about you. You never seem to say much about yourself, and I like that. Most men do nothing but talk about themselves. You seem like you really care about what I have to say. But I doubt I'll ever get to know you completely."

"What is there to know? I am, in many ways, a simple man."

"Oh yeah, sure you are! You run deep, baby. You run real deep."

"And you? Are you a simple woman?"

"Hell no, I'd like to believe I'm a complicated person," laughed Callie. "Too damn mysterious to figure out, but then again, I know I'm not. Hell, life's complicated enough without me making it any harder."

"Speaking of making it harder, look at this," said Darkside, indicating that he was ready for another sexual escapade.

"My, my, my you sure know how to please a girl, don't you?"

The Matriarch of the Seas announced her departure from St. Martin Bay at six o'clock that evening, as the sun began its slow descent into the depths of the Southern Caribbean. Darkside, waiting for Callie to finish dressing for dinner, stood on the top deck watching the enormous ship back out from its mooring birth into the harbor before turning about and heading into the path of the setting sun.

Beautiful, he thought, as he took a deep breath of the clean ocean air.

Realizing that in all the years he'd worked for the royalty of Karoumi, he'd never allowed himself a vacation, he began to wonder why. He'd certainly earned the right to a vacation, but the more he thought, the more he realized that he also never allowed himself the pleasure of a companion. His only human companions were the sheikh, Sela, or the men who worked the horses. Aside from an occasional hooker, he'd never allowed himself the pleasure of knowing a woman. Not like Callie. And he began to ask himself why?

Why have I never allowed a woman into my life? Is it that I do not like them? Or is it that I do not trust them?

He thought of his childhood. He'd been born in a Turkish brothel after his mother, in her last month of pregnancy, had flown to Ankara to confront his father, the diplomat. She was then arrested and thrown into a female prison where he'd been born. He'd been raised by prostitutes until he and his mother were released late one night and flown to Karoumi aboard a Turkish Army DC3. They never knew who or what was responsible for their escape.

But why would that make me not trust women? He

thought. *If anything, I should not trust men.*

The more he thought about his life, the more he realized that he didn't have a woman beside him because his chosen lifestyle didn't allow it. He was always on the road, with the buying, selling, and breeding schedules of the bloodstock. He was up long before dawn and worked non-stop until long after the sun went down, seven days a week. The thing that surprised him most was that he loved it and wouldn't change it for anything. But, that was before he met Callie, and he was fairly sure that those things in his life were about to change.

"Madam," he asked, as he opened the cabin door, "are you ready?"

"Oh yeah," said Callie, her red hair pulled back in a tight bun much like the way she'd worn it the night of the Robard party.

"Good," said Darkside. "I am famished."

It was the night that lobster and filet mignon graced the menu, along with smoked salmon duet, chilled lemon soup with mint leaves, salade melange, veal cordon bleu, garlic rigatoni, and crepes florentine.

They'd eaten like royalty enjoying each other's company enormously, talking and laughing throughout the meal, before Sid signaled the waiter with the after-dinner liqueur.

"No," said Darkside. "This one's on me."

"Okay, if that's the way you want it."

"Tell me, my good man, what is your flavor tonight?"

"Tonight, I am serving what is called an Italian Stallion."

"Please, we will have six. Now then," said Darkside, having signed the check for the liqueur, "allow us to toast each other's health and another good day at sea."

The sextet downed their after-dinner drinks before breaking up, Callie and Darkside making their way to the Promenade deck. The moon laid a perfect path of shimmering diamonds before them as the ship headed westward toward the island of Antigua, 88 nautical miles away.

"The light from the moon on the water makes me think of

home," said Darkside. "which reminds me, I should call..."

"Not now, baby, it's too romantic out here. You'll have plenty of time to do that. Besides, they will just want you to come home or do something other than be here with me," she pouted.

That was probably correct. Since Darkside did not tell anyone where he was going, the people at home, including the sheikh, would probably be disappointed in his carelessness. Even though this was the first time he'd ever done anything like this, he didn't like to disappoint.

"They will worry about me. They are not used to me going off without telling them."

"Maybe it's good that they should worry every now and then. Let them worry."

Although he did think she was being a bit careless in her thinking, he dismissed it with the gentle breeze that blew through his hair and his heart. The scent of the ocean made him think of the time he rode the ferry up the Marmara Sea en route to visit his father. He wanted to know his father, or at least he thought he did. He wanted his father to know him and to love him; but most of all he wanted his father's name.

He remembered the reunion and the wonderful time he had during his visit that year. But even more vividly he remembered how awful life became after he'd left his father's home, when he was arrested and thrown into that stinking Turkish prison. The cause of what had happened to him was never really proven. All he ever knew was that he'd gone to visit his father and, while returning, he'd been arrested. He refused to believe it was his own flesh and blood who'd planted the hash the police had found on him, but he often wondered why the man who had treated him so well, just days before the arrest, had never come to his aid.

He remembered how quickly the trial had flown by and how terribly he was treated the years he'd spent in prison. He remembered how that disgusting prison guard, Nazr the Nazi, had abused and tortured him, forcing him to perform the most vile and demeaning sexual acts. The heartless reprobate would laugh and become aroused while Darkside screamed in pain, begging for mercy. The more screaming, the more laughter, and the more laughter, the more Nazr would become aroused until the filthy, fat monster would tear Darkside's clothes off before viscously violating him.

The wicked guard would often resort to strapping him down across a metal table, while placing a plastic bag over his head. Nazr would then slowly strangle Darkside until the demonic episode would culminate with Nazr's frenzied ejaculation and Darkside spending the next several days in solitary confinement. It seemed that the more pain Nazr could inflict on his helpless victims, the more he enjoyed it. Darkside tried to come to terms with the depths of evil, but it was impossible for a sane man to comprehend. His mind was lost in a collage of long-past memories, as Callie tried recapturing his attention. The past had been brutal, but this moment was the antidote.

"Hey, where are you?" she asked.

"You are right," he agreed with a smile. "Let them worry."

Chapter 15

Wednesday morning found the Matriarch of the Seas docked in the West Indies port of St. John's Bay, Antigua, as the bright Caribbean sun woke the lovers on their third day at sea. And what a beautiful day it was, the ocean breezes jostling the leaves of the tall palm trees hovering protectively above and about the bay. Stepping from the gangway to the concrete pier, Callie remarked just how good she felt.

"You look lovely," said Darkside, kissing her cheek.

Taking a deep breath she said, "Can't you just smell the beauty of it all?"

"Yes, I can smell you, madam."

"Now don't start with that madam stuff again."

They strolled, hand-in-hand through the numerous shops before Callie caught sight of a beautiful emerald and diamond ring.

"Oh my God, look at that!"

"May I help you?" asked a dark-skinned lady with a gleaming gold tooth.

"May I see that ring, please? I just want to see it."

Placing the ring on her finger, she said, "Oh my."

Noticing how her green eyes sparkled and how her voice reminded him of a child at play, he knew that she'd found something that had struck her fancy.

"What is the price?" he asked.

The sales lady looked at the small tag attached to the ring and went to her notebook.

"$3,200, American."

"Too much," said Callie, taking the ring from her finger and placing it on the counter.

"I have more rings over here. Do you prefer emeralds or diamonds?"

"No, I'll just look around, thank you."

Darkside noticed her glancing back at the ring several times while looking around the shop. Without saying anything, he winked at the sales lady.

"What is your lowest price for the ring?" he whispered, as Callie walked out of ear-shot.

"I could come down to 28, but that is as low as I can go."

"25 and you have a deal," said Darkside, placing his Visa card on the counter.

Looking at him and then over at Callie she nodded her approval. Placing his finger to his lips, he indicated that he wanted the transaction to go unnoticed.

Within moments they were toasting each other under the awning of a local rum vendor when he eased the ring box slowly out of his pocket. Pointing to a local bird and exclaiming, "Look at the beautiful colors," he quickly placed it on the table in front of her.

Turning back, she looked at him over top of her sunglasses saying, "I don't know, honey. Looks like a parrot, but I could be wrong."

He didn't say a word, as she placed the straw of her drink into her mouth taking a long sip while glancing down at the ring sparkling beautifully in the mid-morning sun.

"You didn't!" She cried, almost choking.

Placing it on her finger, she looked at him with the innocence of a child. With tears welling she tried to speak but could not.

Darkside, smiling at her, said softly, "For you, madam, for you."

The remainder of the day followed tenderly as the two walked slowly back to the ship for an afternoon of sunbathing, calypso music, and Margueritas before heading to their room to prepare for dinner. Feeling like the world was theirs and looking the part, they strolled into the huge dining room as though they were floating on air.

"Good evening," said their head-waiter, dressed in his black formal slacks, burgundy and white jacket, crisp white shirt, and black bow-tie.

"And how was your day in the West Indies?"

They took their seats while the waiter snapped and unfolded the starched white napkins perched on their dinner plates before laying them gently on each of their laps. Just then the wine steward walked by, and Darkside waved at him.

"Yes, sir, some wine tonight?"

"Yes, we would like a bottle of your finest Merlot."

"Yes, sir, allow me to choose for you," said the wine steward, placing two crystal glasses in front of them.

"Baby," said Callie, "you're a man after my own heart."

"Here you are, sir," said the steward, as he presented the wine.

He uncorked the expensive bottle, and poured a tiny portion into Darkside's glass.

"That is so good," said Darkside. "You may pour the wine."

Lifting his glass toward Callie, Darkside said, "And to us."

Seated in the upstairs dining room, that evening was Lorenzo Groselli, and his partner Wanda Scaranzano from Miami. Wanda, a striptease dancer and call-girl, worked the fancy clubs of Miami Beach. Groselli, a pimp, officially reported to a well-known mob family, but had, in recent years, become more of a liability due to his enormous ego. Rumor had it that he'd become too impatient and ruthless with his women, often requiring them to perform disgraceful, demeaning acts of sexual savagery for his own enjoyment. His mistreatment and infamous temper often scarred a woman for life. If one of the ladies didn't do what she was told, he'd punish her by taking out his frustration on the hapless woman's face. The powers that be, inside the ranks of organized crime, usually don't interfere with the running of the street, so long as the money rolls in, but Groselli had crossed the line of good judgment too many times. He had to go.

Wanda, having coaxed Groselli into taking the cruise by

enticing the self-indulgent Italian with memories of just how good she was in bed, convinced him that he was due a vacation. He didn't know that travelling on board, disguised as a family from New Jersey, were Vinny Grazano and Sonny "Loose Change" Luccachio, hit-men contracted to provide Groselli, in Wanda's own words, "a deep sea solution."

"Lorenzo, I've got some wild friends who want to meet up with us later," whispered Wanda to Groselli as the dinner menus were presented. "Whadda ya say we all get naked and get in a pile later?"

"Hey, baby, that's just fine wit me," responded Groselli.

"Okay, we're gonna meet up with them after the show, up in that big round bar at the back of the ship. What's it called again?"

"You mean that Viking Crown Lounge?"

Back at Callie and Darkside's table, the waiter was describing his choice of delicacies for the evening meal.

"For tonight's appetizer, I suggest the mushrooms Feuilletée, followed by the Oxtail broth and the Ceasar salad. For the main entrée, I suggest the duck á L'Orange and for the dessert, the chocolate soufflé."

"I think the mushrooms sound good, but I'd rather have the shrimp cocktail and the chilled pear soup," said Callie.

"Very good, and for your main entrée?"

"Since tonight is the captain's gala dinner, I think I'm going to have the filet mignon Madagascar."

"An excellent choice, and for you, sir," speaking to Darkside.

"I will have the mushrooms, the salad, and the grilled Norwegian salmon."

"Thank you, sir."

"Oh my," said Sarah, pointing to Callie's ring. "Is that new?"

"Why, yes," she said proudly, holding it up for everyone to see.

"What is it with women and jewelry?" asked Kyle,

jokingly. "I remember when I gave Sarah her engagement ring. Lord have mercy did she squeal."

They joked and laughed toasting each other cheerfully until the waiter handed out the dessert menus.

"And now for dessert we have the chocolate soufflé as well as key lime pie. We have rum and raison ice-cream as well as an apple turnover. We also have New York style cheesecake with fresh raspberries or strawberries. And a low-fat Napoleon which has crisp layers of puff pastry filled with delicate low-fat vanilla custard, accompanied by a tangy Grand Marnier flavored strawberry coulis."

"Here we go again," said Callie, "decisions decisions."

They finished their meal and walked out about the Promenade deck before heading toward the center of the ship and the huge Sound of Music Lounge.

"Who's playing tonight?" asked Callie to the waitress as she placed the Rum Collins on the table.

"I believe they're called The Fifth Dimension."

"Wow, haven't heard from them in quite some time. You're gonna love them, they were popular back in the late sixties."

"What songs did they do?" asked Darkside.

"I think they did 'Aquarius.'"

They thoroughly enjoyed the show and afterward made their way into the casino to play the slot machines, just as Wanda and Lorenzo went to the back of the ship and up to the Viking Crown Lounge.

"Hey, Wanda," called Brea Marelli, as she and Lorenzo came through the lounge doors. "Over here."

"Hey, this here's Lorenzo. This is Brea and Vinny and this here's Jan and Sonny. Some friends from Tampa I told you about."

"You didn't tell me you had friends comin' on dis boat," said Lorenzo, surprised.

"Oh yeah, well, I do and they are, so let's live a little."

"Waitah," said Sonny, in a loud Northeastern accent, "get

ova heah."

They ordered several rounds of drinks, each pretending to enjoy the evening before Lorenzo, having finished his fourth Martini, excused himself to visit the bathroom.

"Now?" asked Sonny.

"Now," answered Wanda.

With that, Sonny walked to the bar and ordered a round of drinks. Signing the receipt, he waited until the bartender had turned his back before he emptied the contents of the black capsule into the Martini. Following Lorenzo back to the table, Sonny placed the drinks down proposing a toast.

"To the good life," he said taking a long pull from the bottle of beer he'd ordered, keeping his eye on Lorenzo the whole time.

"Yeah, the good life," answered Lorenzo.

The effects of the drug didn't hit him all at once. It was more of a gentle feeling that overtook Lorenzo's body as the ship, which had encountered some rough seas, listed and rocked through the midnight water, 70 miles north of St. Lucia.

"Say, I'm fein' pre gud," laughed Lorenzo, as the feeling in his legs disappeared and his speech began to slur.

"How's it hangin' there, dude?" asked Wanda, enjoying the last moments of Lorenzo's life.

"Ha, how good can you swim?" asked Sonny.

"Now don't be messin' with my main man here," teased Vinny, playfully tapping Lorenzo's leg.

After the drug had ample time to render Lorenzo completely helpless, Vinny and Sonny grabbed Lorenzo's arms, and the six of them made their way to the elevator, singing and laughing as though they were having a good time. With almost no one left in the lounge, the group descended three floors making their way to the outer deck towards the back of the ship where there was a clear drop to the water. With the decks empty of guests due to the rough seas and rain that was beginning to fall, Wanda walked to the port-side of the stern and nodded her head approvingly.

Vinny and Sonny looked back toward the starboard side where Janette was stationed. With a positive gesture from her and from Brea, who'd placed herself inside the aft doorway, Vinny and Sonny lifted Lorenzo up and over the railing. The force of the fall from the eleventh deck snapped the mobster's neck as his head hit the water first, killing him instantly.

"Anybody feel like celebrating?" asked Wanda.

"We better split up, and keep to ourselves from here on in," said Sonny.

"So, guess we won't see you again, huh?" asked Janette.

"Guess not. I'm getting off tomorrow morning. Hey, thanks, guys. You don't know what you've done for me and the city of Miami," said Wanda.

"Hey, don't mention it. Rats like him are always screwing things up for the rest of us."

The following morning found Wanda up early to watch the Matriarch pull into St. Lucia. She left the ship unnoticed, hopping into one of the local taxies parked at the end of the pier.

"Good morning, ma'am," said the driver.

"Get me to the airport. I've got a plane to catch."

Chapter 16

Their evening had blended into a symphony of cocktails followed by strategic trips to the cabin for lines of cocaine and interludes of sexual fantasy until, having worn themselves out, they fell into a blissful slumber. They'd slept beyond their call to breakfast and well into mid-morning before the knock on the cabin door forced them from their sleep.

"Excuse please, towels?"

"No, we're fine," answered Callie.

"So sorry."

As the romantic couple stumbled from the bed, Darkside noticed that his cell phone had fallen from the inside of his jacket pocket and was lying on the floor. Without realizing that he was watching, Callie quickly shoved the phone into one of the pockets of her robe hanging behind the door.

That's strange, he thought. Why would she do that?

"How 'bout some lunch," she asked, looking around and seeing Darkside squinting at her.

"That would be nice."

"Well, come on then, let's get this day started off right," she said, handing him the mirror upon which she'd parceled out two wide strips of cocaine.

He took the silver snorting tube from the mirror inhaling the entire line of white powder. Snorting her line in much the same manner, her eyes sparkled as her mouth broke into a slow, almost evil smile.

"Now, that's more like it," she said.

They threw on their clothes, and charged into the main section of the ship, where the large central elevator whisked them up to the Windjammer Cafe and lunch. Following Callie through the buffet line, Darkside felt the dryness in his nostrils caused by the cocaine.

"I am so dry," he said, loading his plate with sea bass and fresh fruit.

"That's part of it. When we get back to the room, I have something for that."

"How about you? Can I just take a big bite of you? Is that good for me?"

"Ha, are you kidding? All you can eat," laughed Callie, selecting a glass of iced tea and making her way to a table along the side railing.

"Now this is beautiful," he said, looking out at the St. Lucia harbor. "I could live here."

"Could you live with me?" she asked, half-kidding and half-serious.

Studying her for a long moment he finally said.

"Do you think you could live with me?"

"Yes, I do."

"Why, you hardly know me. I might be a very mean man."

"I know you. Don't ask me how, but I do. I know you well enough."

Finishing their lunch, they returned to the cabin. It was there that Darkside asked for his cell phone.

Taken somewhat aback by his request, Callie asked, "What's the matter? Need to call for help?"

"Just want to check my messages."

"Baby, baby, let's don't tempt the fates," she said with a mock frown on her face. "Let's just stay right here in our own little world, you and me."

Before he could say anything, she was holding one of her enormous breasts playfully, causing him to change his mind.

"Let's take another hit of this nose candy and get serious," whispered the red-haired vixen, following several long, slow kisses.

It was later that evening as Callie relaxed humming to herself in the shower when, waiting for just the right moment, Darkside went looking for his cell phone. To his astonishment, it was nowhere to be found. But I saw her put it here, he thought, before looking through the dresser drawers containing her clothes.

Pulling her suitcase from beneath the bed, he rummaged around inside. It was there he found the collapsible phone tucked inside a small cosmetic bag in the zippered pouch on the side of the suitcase meant to hold her personals. With the phone in hand he quickly made his way to the top of the ship where he tapped the on/off button. Noticing that the power light failed to turn on, he opened the battery casing where he discovered, much to his chagrin, that the batteries had been removed. With his temper flaring, he walked quickly to the ship's store and purchased the batteries necessary to re-charge his phone. Dialing the number of his answering service, he paced along the deck before realizing that he was too far away to complete the connection.

Rushing to the purser's desk he was instructed to use the guest phone. Standing near the large deck windows on the port side of the ship, he could tell that they'd left St. Lucia, and were several miles out to sea. He dialed the number of his answering service, hearing, "Welcome to Global, Incorporated; you have 24 new messages."

Retrieving his newest message, he couldn't believe his ears as Najema's frantic voice crackled through the phone.

"Sasha, this is Najema. The sheikh has been kidnapped. Please, if you get this message, call me at once."

Fumbling frantically he dialed Najema's office number. After several moments, he heard the warm, familiar voice of the sheikh's personal secretary.

"Sasha. Where are you?"

"I am on a cruise ship. What has happened?"

"Oh, Sasha," sobbed Najema, "the sheikh has been kidnapped. They are holding him ransom for ten-million dollars. When will you be home?"

"Very soon."

"We must pay the money by tomorrow."

"I will be there as soon as possible."

Walking back to the purser's desk, Darkside inquired about their next port-of-call.

"That will be, oh yes, Barbados," replied the tall girl dressed in a white uniform.

"And what time will we dock?"

"We should be in at approximately nine o'clock in the morning."

"Will I be able to get a flight out of there?"

"Yes sir. Is there a problem?"

"No. But thank you."

He hustled to the cabin and, looking hard into Callie's eyes, demanded his cell phone. Seeing his face as a cold mask, she didn't recognize this man. Her blood ran cold as her lower lip quivered while her eyes widened. Looking like a child who'd seen a ghost, she said meekly, "I, I think it's under the bed."

"So did I. And that's just where I found it. Now! Do you want to tell me what is going on?"

Callie knew that this was not the time for concocting a fictional story. She'd been paid a lot of money to get him out of the way, even though she didn't know why. However, with the intense look on his face, she thought it best to admit what she'd done and come clean, not so much for fear of him, but for fear of losing him. She was falling for the guy, and she couldn't help herself. Coming clean might be the only way to keep him.

"Sit down. I have something to tell you," she said, lighting a cigarette. "You're not going to like this, baby, and neither do I, but so help me God. It's the truth."

Seeing the depth of expression on her face, he sat on the bed as she explained how she'd been paid $100,000.00 to romance him and get him out of the way. She usually didn't allow herself to develop feelings for the men she'd fleece, but she told him that this time things had been different and that she was truly enjoying his company.

"But why?" he asked. "Why did you do it? Did you not think it was wrong?"

"I don't know why. I wish I knew. I was a different Callie, a very different Callie for a long time before we met. I can't lie. I've run scams on men before, and this one seemed fairly harmless, but now?"

She stopped long enough to gather herself and take a deep breath before continuing.

"Have you ever done anything you've regretted? Have you ever done something you wished you could undo as though it never happened? But then we wouldn't have been together these last few days. I just wanted to be with you."

Moved by Callie's obvious regret, he waited several moments before asking.

"Do you know my sheikh?"

"I don't know him, but I know of him. I know he's a very kind man. Why?"

"He has been kidnapped."

"Oh," she gasped, placing her hand over her mouth. "No!"

"I must return at once."

"Oh, baby, please. Please don't think I had anything to do with that. Please!"

"Right now it is not important what I think. I must return to my country."

Feeling ashamed, Callie sat down beside him, stroking his tense hand.

"I don't know what to say. I am so sorry. But you must know I didn't know anything like this would happen. I would never do anything to hurt your sheikh. From what I hear, he is good to his people. I would never do anything to harm a man like that."

He tried to listen, but the more he heard, the angrier he became, until finally, "How could you do this to me? How?"

He glared at her as she grabbed her purse and ran out.

Pulling out the small suitcase he'd brought with him and throwing the few clothes he'd had, minus the things she'd bought him, he made his way to the top of the ship where he remained through the night.

It was early when Darkside stumbled down toward the gangway. He'd been watching the island of Barbados coming closer and couldn't wait to disembark.

In the central lobby, Callie caught a glimpse of the man she thought she loved as he crossed the gangway, heading for the cab stand. Rushing to intercept him, she caught him just as he hailed a cab.

"Sasha, you must listen to me," she cried, tears rolling down her blotchy cheeks. "I don't want us to leave like this."

"And how should I leave it?" he demanded. "You have caused me much trouble."

"I know I have, baby, but haven't you ever done anything that you've regretted? Haven't you ever wanted to undo something, but couldn't? Haven't you ever been ashamed of yourself?"

He lingered a few moments looking off in the distance, realizing that, in fact, he had done something he'd long regretted. He couldn't think about that now, not with his sheikh in trouble. Not wanting to look at her, he hopped in the cab and slammed the door, leaving her sobbing inconsolably.

She made her way to one of the park benches under the tall palm trees gently swaying in the morning sun. The penetrating realization engulfed her, forcing her to accept the fact that she'd spent the past week with the love of her life. A man who'd just walked out as quickly as he'd walked in. For the better part of an hour she sat motionless, her mind reeling through the sordid memories of her storied life. She'd thought she'd long since forgotten but realized, to her chagrin that she had not.

Damn men, she thought, trying to force him out of her mind. *Why did he have to leave? Why?*

"Sasha," she called out softly, bending over and hiding her face in her hands. "Come back, come back to me. Please, come back."

Removing her compact from her purse, she dried her eyes, touched-up her makeup, and walked inside the welcome center. Seeing the bottles of duty-free liquor on display, she bought a quart of bourbon for the return trip. Carrying the newly purchased bottle like a newborn baby, she walked slowly back to the ship. With her sunglasses shielding her eyes, she smiled at the attendant as she crossed the gangway.

"Enjoy your day," said the handsome young man in the immaculate white uniform.

I wish I could, she thought. *I only wish I could.*

Darkside was feeling better about himself as his return trip began with good fortune, having arrived at the Barbados airport just in time to board an Egyptian flight bound for Cairo. Once in the air, he wrestled with himself about the fling he'd had with Callie promising Allah that he would never again allow himself to become so irresponsible.

She was some lady, and he knew that forgetting about her was going to be a challenge. She'd kindled a flame in his heart that was going to be very difficult, if not impossible to extinguish. Did he love her? How could he not? But then how could she have done what she did?

I will not think any more of this. I have more important things about which to think.

Chapter 17

On the other side of the world, Darkside's sheikh was also being held on a sea-going vessel. In his case, though, the ship was much less luxurious and his captors much less attractive.

He was several levels down and completely alone when he began to awake. The Knights of the Caliphate had placed him in the captain's quarters toward the back of a second ancient oil tanker, Chrixus, purchased for salvage along with the Galeos. Regaining consciousness, he tried piecing together who and where he was. With the light of a lone 60 watt bulb attached to the wall over the bed to which he was chained, he began to make out his shadowy surroundings.

Thinking he'd died and resurfaced within the confines of his own karmic solitude, his mind played tricks on him, as his nostrils filled with the sour smells of rusted metal and dank, stagnant air. Pulling against the long chain tethering him to the bed, he realized that, no matter how hard he tried, he wasn't going anywhere. Uncharacteristically, and with disdain, he reclined on the bed, closing his eyes while he prayed. He didn't pray for himself; he prayed for the others, so that they wouldn't be distraught when they realized he was gone. The only thing missing was that he couldn't remember exactly who the others were. He knew his life was in danger and that his chances of ever seeing his home again were nil, but he didn't know why. Not only that, he couldn't remember where his homeland was.

Trying desperately to conjure memories and establish a link to his past, the harder he tried, the less he could envision. He vaguely remembered that he'd had a brother who had always hated him. He asked himself if his predicament could have anything to do with that?

Could this be the culmination of Rajad's hatred toward me? He thought.

Allowing his mind to search back through time in an effort to understand what had fueled the fiery dislike that had raged within Rajad's heart, he lay on the bed groping through the past. His foggy mind slightly remembered how their mother had died while he and his father had been away on a falconry expedition. He remembered how a very young Rajad, having witnessed the last moments of his mother's life, had lain next to her body for days before being discovered.

But what did that have to do with me? He thought. *I was not responsible for Mother's death. I was away with Father.*

He searched his mind in vain until it dawned on him.

That's it! It was always me and Father. It was never me and Father and Rajad. It was never Rajad and Father. And it was never Rajad and me. It was just me and Father without Rajad. He grew up without us, even though we could not see it. He was never with us. He was always alone.

How things between them had grown so bad was beyond his ability to comprehend, and his mind was very confused. Lying helpless on the dirty bed, he remembered how depressed he was during that period of his life. So many things had happened so quickly, so many new faces. How much he'd missed his father, the true mentor in his life.

Sasha! He thought. What about Sasha?

He remembered what had caused him to admire the handsome man with the birthmark on his face. It was his undying loyalty and total devotion to Rajad while Rajad was alive. He remembered his first real encounter with Darkside following Rajad's death and the tender words Rajad had spoke kneeling before his newly adorned sheikh. With tears streaming down his cheeks he whispered softly, "My life is your life, my sheikh. I live only to serve you. I will serve and protect you as you have served and protected us for so very long."

With his short-term memory compromised due to the

massive dose of anesthetic, he allowed his long-term memory to entertain and accompany him during this torturous ordeal. One of the more pleasing aspects of those times was how quickly Jules Weherner had disappeared. A truly vicious person, Jules would have stopped at nothing in achieving her incessant ambition. She had her eye on the matriarchal throne and was poised to entice Efram into a love affair, had Darkside not intervened forcing her to leave the country. Efram never knew that it was Jules who master-minded the genetic poison that Darkside had delivered to Kentucky, which had caused so many Thoroughbred foals to be stillborn in 1996. Not only that, but Efram never knew that it was Darkside who facilitated Jules' death, keeping his sheikh safe from her diabolical clutches.

Efram thought about how Darkside had come to love the horses, and how he could often be found at the stables, quietly tending to the needs of the mares and foals, saddling the young fillies and colts for their workouts, as the yellowing dawn chased the guilt of darkness from another innocent morning. Karoumi was beginning to build a sizable stable of horses, and Darkside seemed to revel in its success.

Everyone thought it befitting when the sheikh asked Darkside to accompany him on a trip to Ireland, and their first official Thoroughbred auction. Efram, knowing nothing about running the stables, the horse business, or how to build a breeding and racing establishment, hired two of England's finest horsemen to provide the immediate equine direction Karoumi so desperately needed. Following two years of constant involvement, Darkside had grown to become a solid horseman, with an eye for speed and stamina and a hunger to build the Karoumi Stables into a world-class breeding facility.

He remembered Darkside's face the day he'd asked him to become the director of the facility. Stunned in disbelief, all Darkside could mutter was, "My sheikh, I, I do not know what to say."

"I have been watching you, my friend," said Efram. "You

are quite the horseman. You know as much about the care and welfare of these animals as does anyone. You also know how to buy the right horse and at just the right price. You will be a great asset to your country."

"My life is your life, my sheikh. If that is what you desire of me, then of course, that is what I will do."

Chapter 18

As the long day crept into twilight, the ancient vessel with its precious cargo sat listing far from the nearest road, and 25 miles from Karamurtak, Turkey, along the banks of the Marmara Sea.

"Eat," ordered Kazeem, shaking Efram from his deep sleep.

"Where am I?" he asked weakly, his eyes blinking uncontrollably.

"You have been, how should we say, kidnapped. You are on a boat far from your homeland."

"What are you going to do with me? Are you going to kill me?"

"It depends on the money."

"Money?" asked Efram.

"The ten million dollars."

"And you think I am worth that?"

"Ha," laughed Kazeem. "What do you think?"

"Why do you do this to me? What have I ever done to you?"

"We want only what we are owed."

"And what is that? I recall no such debt!"

"Easy, my friend, you are in no position to demand. It was your brother. He owes us. He failed to pay us what he owed us and he betrayed us."

"Did you kill my brother?" asked Efram innocently, not knowing what, nor who had ultimately caused Rajad's death.

"I did not kill your brother, but I would have. It appears that we were not the only ones who wanted him dead."

"Why did he owe you ten-million dollars?"

"He owed us one-million dollars, but we feel that, for our trouble, you would bring much more than that."

"I do not understand," said Efram.

"He hired us to bomb a plane."

"A plane, what plane?"

"From New York, a plane on which," Kazeem hesitated, "YOU were travelling."

The awful truth hit Efram like a runaway stallion as he sat on the bed staring at the wall. Taking pity on the heartbroken sheikh, the terrorist said, "Eat, you must maintain your strength."

"I am, not hungry," said Efram, leaning over the bed in pain. His intestines had been tied like a bundle of soldered wire ever since he awoke from the anesthetic, and he was beginning to pass blood from his bowels.

"Suit yourself my friend," said Kazeem, with a look of compassion in his eyes. Placing his hand on Efram's shoulder he said, "You must ride with Allah. The bomb was perfect, but for reasons unknown to us, it failed to explode. You are one lucky man, my friend."

With his mouth open in disbelief, the sheikh sat doubled over in pain, unaware of his immediate surroundings. Kazeem left the saddened monarch returning to the large room near the front of the boat.

"We must kill him!" said Ramone, one of Kazeem's henchmen, who'd been posturing to take over the gang for several months. All the Knights knew that Kazeem had been slowing down the last few years, and was tired of living like a vagabond. Many within the unholy group felt that Kazeem no longer burned with the passion to seek the goals of the Knights, but no one had the audacity to approach him about it. Kazeem's eyes could still burn ferociously, and no one doubted his strength.

"We will wait and see," said Kazeem, matter-of-factly.

"I say we kill him," said Ramone.

The other three seemed to favor Ramone's suggestion, but seizing the moment and acting like the strong leader the men always admired, Kazeem retorted, "We will do this my way." Looking into each of their eyes as he said it, the discussion was brought to an abrupt close.

"How much longer?" barked Kazeem.

"13 hours," answered Ramone, disgustedly.

"Then, let us prepare. There must be no mistakes. One mistake and we miss our only chance. If we do not make the pickup, they will think we have killed him and our plans will be foiled."

The men listened intently to Kazeem, having followed him for years, each admiring his master-mindedness when it came to planning illegal activities and avoiding the law.

"I will dress as a tourist. I will purchase a ticket on the ferry and will walk slowly along the Galata Bridge as though I were taking pictures. When I approach the person holding the suitcase, I will take a picture while telling him to put the suitcase down. I will then pick it up and carry it to the ferry. I will probably be watched. If anyone is following me, they will most likely follow me on board the boat.

I must go down to the car deck and walk through the vehicles to the back of the ferry. Ramone, you will be in the runabout and will have the field-glasses on me at all times. When I have made it to the back of the car deck, you will bring the boat in next to the ferry and I will jump in. We should be out of the harbor and over to the Asian side within minutes. During this time, I will move the money from the suitcase into a backpack. This must be completed before we reach the shore."

Continuing his instructions, Kazeem looked to the tall man on the other side of the room.

"Stavrok, you will be waiting with the truck. You must have the motorcycle running. As soon as we arrive, lower the tailgate, and I will put on an overcoat and hat, and ride the motorcycle out of the city. Once we are in the clear, we must be sure we have not been followed. When you and Ramone get to the edge of Karamurtak, ditch the truck and take a bus to within walking distance. We will then meet back here as soon as we can. Remember, we must not be followed."

The men sat mesmerized by the intricacy yet simplicity of the plan. Looking into each man's eyes while he spoke, Kazeem concluded, "Are there any questions?"

"Who carries the backpack?" asked Ramone, as his eyes moved questionably from Kazeem to Stavrok. "Which one of us has that honor?"

"Ramone, my friend," said Kazeem, smiling, "are we not brothers in our cause? Do you not trust your brother? Or expect your brother not to trust you?"

"Ha, brothers, how much trust did that sheikh have in his brother?" asked Ramone disrespectfully.

"Yes, what about him?" asked Stavrok. "How do I know I can trust any of you?"

"We are one within each other, eh?" said Kazeem. "We have always been a team. Why should we stop now? Besides, it will be easier to avoid the authorities on the motorcycle."

"But we have never had ten-million dollars before," stated Ramone.

"So, it is the money, eh?"

"It is always the money."

"Well, I guess we have to take our chances. But think about it. Where would we go? We have survived because we have always remained together. If one of us was to take the money and run, how far would he get, eh? And who would he go to when he needed something? Why would we throw away what little family we have?"

It was a fair question causing the men to reflect on what he'd said.

"Now!" demanded Kazeem, "I will carry the money. Agreed? Good! Then we go."

Chapter 19

The sun was shining, the sky was clear, and it was a perfect day for tourists, as the ferry boats came and went from the Galata Bridge in Istanbul. It was five minutes to four in the afternoon, as the courier with the suitcase made his way to the center of the bridge.

Kazeem, dressed in beige shorts, a short-sleeved shirt resembling an American flag, white socks, tennis shoes, and a New York Yankees cap turned backwards, walked slowly across the bridge taking pictures of the ships docked nearby. Approaching the man with the suitcase, he could see how nervous he was. Walking up beside him with his camera to his eye, Kazeem asked, "Do you have the key to this suitcase?"

Without saying a word, the man gestured nervously that he did not know.

"Place the suitcase down and walk away," ordered Kazeem, in a stern, but quiet voice.

The nervous man dropped his burden and disappeared.

Kazeem recovered the suitcase and walked briskly toward the ferryboats docked at the pier. Handing in his boarding pass, he made his way along the main deck toward the rear of the boat. Hustling down two flights of stairs to where the cars were driving in, he walked briskly over to the far side of the loading platform. Arriving just in time, Ramone swooped in with the runabout. They were off to the Asian side of Istanbul, before anyone knew what had happened.

"How does it look?" shouted Ramone, as Kazeem stuffed the money in the backpack.

"Ha ha we are rich, we are rich."

It all went perfectly, the pickup, the get-away, the transfer to the motorcycle, and now all they had to do was get back to the ship, kill the sheikh, and find their way into hiding for another long, arduous stay. But as Kazeem gunned his Kawasaki 400 he had second thoughts. He was getting older and it was time he settled down. Possibly with Anya, a woman with whom he'd had a fling several years ago. Now that he had the money, maybe he could rekindle the feelings he once had for her. He wanted out of the Knights and now he had the fortune to do it.

What can stop me now, he thought. *Nothing! Nothing but the life of a gentle, mild-mannered man, tethered to a bunk deep within the hull of a rusted-out oil tanker. Am I developing a conscience?*

Ramone and Stavrok found their way to Chatrak where they ditched the truck. On a lonely stretch of road outside the city of Yalova, they vanished into the nearby forest.

Having raced the entire way back to the ship, Kazeem parked the bike, climbed down into the hold, and pitched the overstuffed backpack onto a table.

"Look at this," he said, pulling a handful of money out. "We are rich. We are filthy, stinking rich."

"Where are the others?" asked Ab, with a puzzled look on his face.

"To hell with the others, look at what we have here."

"What do you mean?"

"I mean, what do we need with them? We have enough here to live happily for the rest of our lives," said Kazeem, throwing handfuls of money in the air.

"I do not like how that sounds. Are we a team or not?" demanded Ab.

Flashing a demonic look toward Ab, Kazeem said, "On which side of this team are you?"

"I, I am on your side."

"Good, then take your money and run."

"What about him?" asked Ab, pointing toward the stairs leading down to the sheikh. He sensed something different about the leader of the group and thought he'd been acting strange lately.

"I will take care of him. Here, take this," said Kazeem, handing Ab several handfuls of money. "This is all you will need. Go and take care of yourself."

"Where will you go? And why are you in such a hurry? Are you going to kill him or not?"

"Do not be concerned with me. Think about yourself. You must go into hiding. Or better yet, leave the country. Go back to Iran or maybe to sea."

"What about the others?"

"Just take care of yourself."

Shoving several handfuls of money in a gunny sack, Ab looked at Kazeem as if to say something, then turned running up the stairway.

Kazeem descended the stairs to where Efram lay tethered to the stateroom bed. He could hear the helpless sheikh vomiting violently. Seeing him in extreme distress, he reached out to help the man who'd soiled himself causing a foul stench to permeate the room. Kazeem dropped to his knees opening the wineskin of water dangling from his shoulder. Pouring it on Efram's face and neck, he asked, "What has happened to you?"

Releasing him from his chains, Kazeem handed Efram an old shirt and a pair of dingy, worn slacks, he said, "Put these on. They are not clean, but they will do you well."

"I am ill," said Efram, in a thin, hollow voice.

"That, I can see. You do not look well, my friend. I can only imagine how you must feel. But I have the money, my good sheikh, and I must now deal with you."

Having pulled himself to stand before his kidnapper, Efram said, "Please, if I must die, allow me to die in my own clothing. If I truly am a sheikh, then that is how I would prefer to look during my own death."

"Clean yourself," ordered Kazeem, "you will die someday, my friend, but not this day."

With a disgusted look, the sheikh slowly removed his

kingly robes. Cleaning himself as well as he could, he dressed in the clothes Kazeem had given him.

"Well now, my good sheikh. Shall we go?"

"Where?"

"Do not ask. It would be in your best interest if you did not know."

Helping the sheikh up the stairs, Kazeem retrieved his motorcycle, kick-starting it until it came alive with a noisy roar.

"Grab the backpack," he ordered.

The men mounted the vibrating machine and rode into the darkness, with Efram holding on for dear life. Having caused several untimely stops throughout the night, Efram blinked his tired eyes as the morning sun peeked over the distant mountains, blinding him temporarily. Pulling off at a gas station, Kazeem helped him into the bathroom. After refueling the bike and refreshing themselves, the two were once again headed eastward as fast as the bike could carry them.

"Where are we to go?" asked Efram, straining to be heard above the sound of the engine.

"I am taking you to where I know you will be safe."

"You are not going to kill me?"

"Do I look like a murderer to you? Well maybe I do. Ha, if I didn't kill your brother, do you think I would kill you?"

For the first time in several days, Efram's digestive system began to relax, and the gripping pains he'd felt in the pit of his stomach began to ease. Once again he could feel the hand of Allah resting gently on his shoulder. He didn't know what was happening to him, or why, but he did know that he was experiencing the adventure of his life.

Chapter 20

Anya Gurbuz stirred the rabbit stew in the large black-iron caldron hanging over the smoldering coals of a week-long fire. She was in the waning years of her fourth decade, showing the age of hardship as her semi-dark hair, streaked with wisps of white and yellow-gray, hung to her shoulders.

She was the daughter of a moderately wealthy Turkish aristocrat but had left home at an early age to attend Ankara University. It was there that she'd met and had fallen in love with Tobarek Kazeem, the handsome, brash rebel and eventual leader of the notorious Knights of the Caliphate.

With her liberal political attitude, Anya had become captivated by the charming ways of Kazeem. He was intelligent and well-versed in ghetto life, and taught her the ways of the street.

Thinking that the Knights were on a mission from Allah, she'd allowed him to become not only her hero, but the man to whom she would devote herself. Eventually, the cause lost its luster as Anya realized that they were doing much more harm than good. The end came when she'd become involved with the bombing of a village bistro, where torturous ordeals of police brutality were known to have taken place. Through her friend, Sulag, she'd witnessed the horrific goings-on and was determined to help destroy the unholy establishment.

She liked Sulag, a friendly, happy-go-lucky student whose only crime had been being seen at the wrong place and with the wrong people. The 19 year-old engineering student had suffered from a mild birth defect which had left him partially crippled, causing him to walk with a distinct limp and to use a cane. This, along with his wonderful sense of humor, is why the rebel group avoided him, not wanting to be part of the attention he always seemed to attract. But Anya was his friend and he was often seen in her company.

It was Sulag's misfortune that he was abducted by the Turkish underground police one evening while returning home from an arduous day of mid-term exams. Believing him to be a member of the rebel group, the police placed Sulag's fingers inside the infamous "Satan's glove," a medieval torture device. Held by this wretched apparatus for days, and unable to withstand the excruciating pain, Sulag finally told the militia what they wanted to know. He had indeed known about the bistro bombing. Whether he was part of the responsible group or not, his captives would not relent until he broke.

"You must run. They know," said a sobbing Sulag, as he held onto Anya's arm.

"What do you mean?" she asked.

"I had to tell them. They, they made me. Look! Look at my hands, my hands," he cried.

Anya couldn't believe what she was seeing. Unwrapping Sulag's fingers slowly, her eyes widened in horror as she revealed the grotesque swelling in his fingers, the ends of which were completely black and blue, the fingernails having been pulled out.

"Oh my God," gasped Anya. "Who did this to you?"

"They know who you are. You must run, or they, they will kill you."

"Who are they?"

"The police, the detectives, you know who."

"Did you tell them my name?"

"I, I had to. But you must run. They will kill you. They know who you are. I am sorry. I am so sorry."

Holding Sulag to her breast, she whispered softly in his ear, "It is alright. Do not worry about me; take care of yourself."

The Knights forgave Sulag. It was his curse to know any of them. Angered by his torture, they bombed the building where Sulag had been held, but their actions, fueled by self-righteous passion, caused the deaths of two of Ankara's undercover detectives. What had begun as a mere protest of the political happenings of the times ended with the members of Kazeem's rebels being labeled as criminals of the state who were forced to either flee the country or disappear into hiding. Kazeem and Anya went separate ways, but it was always Anya's opinion that things had turned out for the best.

Determined to make a life for herself outside both the law and her family, Anya, through her wide range of compatriots, was introduced to a small band of Gypsies and had lived among the wandering tribe for the past 20 plus years. With her wealth of matronly qualities, and good-natured disposition, she'd quickly become one of the matriarchs of the tightly knit nomadic group. Frequently called upon to share her ever-growing wisdom, she was often selected to aid in settling the cultural and domestic differences that, from time-to-time, plagued the diverse constituents. She'd often thought about returning to her home, but her communication was always thwarted by the fear of capture and her father's inability to forgive her. Over time, her Gypsy band had become her true family.

They travelled the plains and fields of Turkey, living in a tent village, farming and fishing from one remote area to the next. Their lifestyle, considered strange and almost demonic by many of the more religious members of European society, allowed them to enjoy life to the fullest. They lived by their own rules in a world defined and attuned totally unto themselves.

Gypsies originated more than a thousand years ago in northwestern India, in what was known as the Punjab area. Fleeing from warring Arab and Mongolian factions, they scattered throughout the Middle East to the far reaches of Egypt, where they became known as 'Gypcians'. Many Gypsies today regard themselves as descendents of Egyptian royalty; however, none can formally trace their ancestry to include Egypt or its royalty as their place of origin, especially, the Turks.

Having joined the Gypsies at the tender age of 21, Anya

was now approaching fifty. In all the years living among this energetic, freedom-loving group, she'd never found a husband but, nonetheless was sought by other tribal women to assist in the ritual of virginity assessment. Gypsy tradition dictates that each woman remain a virgin until marriage, and when one of the tribe's young girls presents herself for marriage, a virginity examiner is sent to verify that the hymen of the betrothed is intact. Anya's gentle nature put these young women at ease, so that it did not become a dreaded ordeal. Why Anya hadn't married was never understood. Even though many of the men were attracted to her, very few ever approached her other than to ask her to dance or seek her advice.

A robust woman, healthy, but not too large, she wore her clothes loosely, never tight. Keeping herself very clean, she was not overly concerned with her appearance, allowing her hair to blow as wildly as the breezes which blew through the campsite. She smiled often but seldom laughed out loud. She was sweetly attentive to those around her yet most of the time could be found in deep thought, quietly humming. To her compatriots, she was regarded as a true pleasure to be around.

It was approaching noon when Anya heard the throaty sound of a motorcycle off in the distance. Watching the men on the two-wheeled machine come up the road, down the grassy embankment, and across the field to where she stood, she didn't recognize either of them.

"Anya," called Kazeem, "hey, Anya."

Realizing who it was she broke into a wide smile running gleefully into the arms of her former lover.

"I cannot believe my eyes. What brings you here?"

"I have brought a friend, a sheikh, can you take care of him?" as Efram, unable to stand, fell off the back of the bike.

"A sheikh?"

"Don't ask any questions. He is in trouble and needs help. He is being chased and will be killed if he is found."

"What would you want me to do?"

"Can you look after him for a few days? I will be back

soon. It will only take a few days," said Kazeem, looking around to see if they'd been followed.

"You want to leave him here, with me? I, I..."

"I will return when it is safe. Until then, take care of him. There are bad men after him, and I must go at once."

"Kazeem, wait."

He sped off and out of sight leaving Anya in mid-sentence as Efram lay prostrate on the ground. Calling to a teenage boy standing nearby, they moved the sheikh into her tent, where she removed his shoes, placing him on a pallet she'd quickly thrown together.

Efram slept without stirring for the next several hours, while Anya met with the other members of the group, informing them of what had transpired. Late the next day, Efram stumbled from the tent as the sun was beginning to set, squinting as he made his way toward her.

"Would you like to take a bath and have some clean clothes?" she asked.

He nodded his approval without saying a word.

She heated the water and found some clean clothes, including an old vest she'd kept to remind her of Mustafa, the man she'd lived with for several years. They'd lived quietly and happily until the day he returned from Ankara with news that he had cancer. Unable to afford adequate treatment, he had no choice but to try and outlast the disease which had staked its claim to his body beginning in his testicles.

In less than a year it had spread into his lymphatic system and most major organs, harassing him relentlessly to an untimely and painful death. His last days were spent in delirium, burning with fever and pain, causing him to bite the ends of his fingers until there was nothing left but bloody stubs.

Anya begged Allah to intervene on his behalf, but her prayers went unanswered. Finding no relief for herself or the man she loved, she coped with the ordeal the best she could, force-feeding him potions while continuously bathing his overheated body. The end came as his oxygen-starved remains gave out in the early hours of a beautiful summer morning. Mustafa was laid to rest in grand Gypsy style, after which Anya returned to her campground chores where she'd remained untouched for the past 13 years.

Chapter 21

The 127th running of the Kentucky Derby found 16 horses ready and as fit as any group of entrants in the history of the classic event. Among the field were winning athletes:

Millennium Wind - the Santa Catalina and the heralded Blue Grass Stakes;

Songandaprayer - the Fountain of Youth;

Dollar Bill - the Risen Star Stakes;

Startac - the Turf Paradise Derby;

Monarchos - the Florida Derby;

Fifty Stars - the Louisiana Derby;

Point Given - the San Felipe Stakes, Santa Anita Derby;

Balto Star - the Spiral Stakes and the Arkansas Derby;

Congaree - the Wood Memorial, and

Keats, the Coolmore Lexington Stakes.

Never before had so much speed and class been gathered in Louisville to run for the roses, and Johnny Stone knew it. He'd driven the 80 miles from Lexington before sunup, and had parked near Churchill Downs' famous Backside. He strolled down through the hallowed ground he'd traversed so many times in his past, but today was different. As much as he tried to get excited about the best day in a Kentuckian's life, his heart wasn't in it. Just one day earlier, he'd witnessed a sight that seemed destined for his nightmares. An endless stream of horsemen carrying dead fetuses and stillborn foal corpses lined up at the Kentucky Equine Diagnostic Center. Having been tipped off that a large number of mares were either aborting early, or delivering stillborn foals, he'd driven over to the center to get a first-hand look. He now wished he hadn't.

Johnny'd grown up in the Bluegrass, and for over 50 years had celebrated the greatest two minutes in sports each and every year. No matter where he was or what he was doing, Derby Day, to him, was the best day of the year. The first months of each new year, he'd start watching the three-year-olds stake their claim to the Derby by winning one of the several prep races, which qualified them as entrants. Today he was one of the unfortunate few who knew the truth about what was happening to the animals that drove the entire industry. Even amidst the excited throngs, he couldn't share their enthusiasm. While 150,000 people were sipping their mint juleps and cavorting drunkenly about the infield, 73 of Kentucky's foals would die. It would set a record for foal deaths in one day, marking the worst episode in the history of Thoroughbred breeding. And as bad as it was, it was going to get worse.

The enormous crowd converged on Churchill Downs, as Gwen Gardot and the rest of Dr. Pehlagrem's staff were a few miles away working tirelessly behind the scenes. Their mission had a single focus, to combat the dreaded disease robbing Kentucky of its bloodlines. Having arrived as the sun spread its sweetened glory over the misty morning dew, Gwen brought with her most of the notes she'd taken years earlier. She became immediately helpful in determining the appropriate questions which needed to be asked of the farmers in Central Kentucky.

"Gwen, I want to thank you again for coming on such short notice," said Dr. Pehlagrem. "You don't know how happy I am that you've joined us."

"The way I look at it, we're all in it together, Doctor."

"I love your attitude. Tell me, have you got any suggestions regarding the press? I understand you were pretty instrumental in dealing with them a few years ago."

"The only thing I would suggest is to hold the story until we can rule out a few things. We sure don't need to panic these farmers, especially after what happened in 1996."

"I couldn't agree with you more. But do you think we can get them to wait?"

"I think, if you promise them an exclusive story when we do know something, they'll hold off. But it won't last long."

"That's what I'm afraid of. I just remember how well they wrote about the problems the last time this happened. They were quite respectful and really tried to report the story as favorably as possible."

"Well, that's good to hear. I mean I don't have to tell you that this is Kentucky's number one cash crop."

Chapter 22

Dr. Pehlagrem called a meeting that afternoon to discuss how the staff was going to handle the press. Preparing for the story to break within the next day or two, she wanted them to know what to say and how to handle themselves. She knew that each member of the team was a professional, but the vast majority of doctors and scientists were inexperienced and unaware of the burgeoning intensity the news media could bring. With the task unfolding, she knew that they were facing extremely long hours and wanted to stress that it would be in no one's interest to appear argumentative.

Gwen stopped working just long enough to place a call. The gentle voice of the man she knew from years gone by answered.

"Hello, this is Tuck."

"Tucker, this is Gwen. I'm in Lexington."

"Gee, that was fast. You must have sprouted wings."

"I'm working with Doctor Pehlagrem."

"Well, great. They can sure use an old hand like you."

"Any chance we could get together?" she asked.

"I don't see why not. What's your schedule look like?"

"I know we'll basically be working around the clock, but I could probably slip away for some dinner. That's if you don't have any plans."

"Me, have plans? The only plans I have are all on four legs, and some are about to give birth."

"So have you experienced anymore," she hesitated before asking, "foal deaths?" It was a sensitive topic, but Gwen knew she could be straight with Tuck.

"Not so far, but who knows? I can't believe we had two in one barn."

"That really stinks, you know that?"

"Dang right I know it, worst thing that's happened to Fairhaven since I've been here."

"You know, Tuck, I really do want to see you."

"Yeah, me too, so how's tomorrow night look?"

"Pretty good, just tell me what time you're picking me up."

"How's about seven?"

"Not soon enough, but it'll have to do."

"Okay, where will you be?"

"Here at the center. I'll call and let you know if anything changes, but for right now, I'll be here at the front door at seven sharp."

"That's great, Gwen. I can't wait to see ya."

"Same here, Tuck. It's been a long time."

They'd come together five years earlier in an effort to solve a similar foal-death malady and had formed quite a bond. But time, distance, and their individual careers had reluctantly forced them apart. Or at least that's the way Gwen had interpreted it.

Through hard work and determination, she'd earned her undergraduate degree in biology, her Masters in animal husbandry, and her Doctorate in equine medicine before taking a job at the Kentucky Equine Research Center. With her competitive work ethic and inner self-control, she rarely allowed the alluring, disastrous aspects of romance to sidetrack her, feeling there was more to lose than gain. Until Tuck came along, she'd never realized the true splendors of feeling a heart-to-heart connection.

Having been raised by her grandmother in a small town in Texas, most of her previous heart-rending adventures incorporated mares, foals, and stallions. She was a horse-lover from the time her daddy'd placed her on old Redwing the summer of her third birthday. She could barely remember those short, sweet years when the world was new and her parents were alive, before the tragic accident when she was six years old. Her grandmother was good to her and did the best she could, but something other-worldly seemed to burn within Gwen's soul, a quest that forced her to drive herself to constant over-achievement.

But how often does life provide one a chance at the perfect partner? And when it does, how many chances does one get to accept such good karma? Memories of Tuck haunted the horse woman ever since she'd decided to move away.

He was on her mind more often than she would admit these past five years, especially at night, when the day's work was complete and she'd lie in bed, with only his memory to snuggle. She'd remember how much in common they both had, even though their first encounter was one she would sooner have forgotten. She remembered that phone call in 1996, when the foals were dying at an epidemic rate. She remembered the conversation and could still hear Doc Baich's frantic voice on the phone...

"Gwen, Doc Baich here, I'm over at Fairhaven and, hell Gwen, we've got another one," his voice dropping to a tone beyond sadness.

"Not Kissin' Kouzins?"

"Yeah, Gwen, this thing's bad, real bad. Have you found anything?"

"Doc, the only thing I can tell you is that we're doing everything we can."

"Give me that," said Tuck in a gruff voice, grabbing the phone. As hateful as his voice sounded at the time, it proved to be one of her fondest memories.

"Doctor Gardot, this is Tucker Flannery. I'm the manager of Fairhaven Farm. What the hell are you people doing over there anyway?"

"I can assure you, we are doing everything we can to resolve this situation."

"Situation, is that what you're calling it, a situation? Now they're calling it a situation. Well, we've got more than a goddamn situation here, missy!"

"Believe me, you are not telling me anything I don't already know," her voice somewhere between angry and professional.

"Well, when can WE expect to know something?"

"The moment I know myself," she said through clenched teeth.

"Okay, I uh, well look thanks. I'm sorry, guess I was just," Tuck handed the phone back to Doc Baich and stormed out of the barn.

She remembered meeting Tuck the following afternoon when she went to inspect Kissin' Kouzins' dead foal. It was the way Tuck held out his hand and apologized to her that changed her opinion of him. It seemed that every time she'd close her eyes the last few years, she could see him extending his hand with that sincere, worried look on his face.

"I'm sorry I was so gruff on the phone, Doc. I, ah, I'm not usually like that. This problem we're having has gotten to me, but I should never have talked to you like that. I'm sorry."

Those were some of the kindest words she'd ever heard.

They grew to respect each other and, upon discovering they'd had more than just horses in common, began dating. That is until Gwen was offered the job in Florida, and believing that Tuck's commitment was to the responsibilities of his farm management, decided to follow her professional dreams and move south. But that was then, and after pushing herself these last five years to become one of the equine industry's top scientists, she'd realized that she may have been a bit too hasty. Could fate and these foal deaths have, for a second time in her life, brought her together with the perfect mate? She didn't know for sure, but the one thing she did know was that, if indeed it had, she was not going to let him get away. Not this time.

Chapter 23

Johnny Stone made his way over to the press box to where he could get a good look at the field as it charged toward the clubhouse turn. Usually quite happy in the company of his fellow reporters, he found himself wanting to be alone. He knew his lead story was going to have to be about how the field finished and how the favorites had fared, but his mind wasn't on the business at hand. It was somewhere inside the foaling barns where helpless young animals were suffocating within the bellies of their mothers; mothers hopelessly unable to prevent their babies from suffering a horrible, premature death.

Lowering his head, he allowed his mind to take him to his boyhood and how he would watch the Kentucky Derby on his parent's old black and white Motorola with the signal fading in and out. How many winners had he watched over the years. Horses like Tim Tam who won the Derby and the Preakness before finishing second in the Belmont with a broken sesamoid bone in his leg. And Northern Dancer, the little horse who won the Derby while Johnny was in college. A smile broke over his face as he remembered spending Derby eve as a guest in the Louisville Jail after having smarted off to a pair of policemen who were trying to prevent a race riot from breaking out downtown. But his favorite horse and his favorite Derby was Secretariat in 1973. Secretariat was the most beautiful horse he'd ever seen, and Johnny was quite fortunate to have been in the press box that year covering the race as a cub reporter.

As the afternoon heat turned the overcrowded racetrack into a cauldron of steaming, burning flesh, Johnny loosened his tie and placed his field glasses to his eyes as the first chords of 'My Old Kentucky Home' wafted charmingly in the air. He remained glued to the track until Monarchos stormed down the stretch in a blistering one minute 59 and nine-tenths, the second fastest in Kentucky Derby history, and less than a half second off the immortal Secretariat's time. Thoughts of how he was going to write about the second fastest Derby in history and the fastest track Churchill Downs had ever produced whipped through his mind as hard as did the wind through the open windows of his Cadillac. But no matter what thoughts came to mind, the memory of all those horsemen and the dead foals was simply not going to allow him to enjoy his favorite day of the year.

Chapter 24

Karoumi, in the United Arab Emirates

Darkside's plane touched down in the early morning hours, as the weary traveler sat patiently while the small McDonnell Douglas MD-80 came to a stop near gate three. Najema paced the floor by the large window hoping to catch a glimpse of Darkside as he made his way to the door of the plane. Seeing him come through the gate, she ran ahead of the guards accompanying her to welcome him, bursting into tears while falling into his arms.

"Now, now," said Darkside. "Everything will be fine."

"Oh, Sasha, where did you go? What has happened to our sheikh? What is going on?"

Seeing the guards closing in around him, Darkside knew immediately that he was under suspicion.

"Mr. Prahstomank, we must ask you some questions," said an unknown man dressed in a suit and tie.

"Who are you?" asked Darkside.

"My name is Inspector Edwards, and I am from Interpol."

"Am I under arrest?"

"We must detain you in order to ask you some questions. That's all."

"Where are you taking him?" asked Najema.

Ignoring her question, they left the airport in a drab-green car with Najema following in the sheikh's limousine. Arriving at the municipal station, Inspector Edwards began asking Darkside of his whereabouts during the kidnapping.

"I, I was on holiday."

"I see. And where was this holiday?"

"The Caribbean, we flew to San Juan from Kentucky and went aboard a cruise ship."

"I see, and with whom?"

"A friend I know from Kentucky."

"So you were in Kentucky on business and then went on holiday?"

"I was on business. I did not plan to go on holiday. It just worked out that way."

"Yes, I see. You were on business and then you were on holiday and then the sheikh was kidnapped."

"Do you believe I had something to do with my sheikh being kidnapped?"

"You must admit, it does look a bit suspicious. You go to Kentucky on business, and then the next thing anyone knows is that you cannot be found. No one hears from you and then the sheikh is kidnapped. You then call from somewhere out on the Caribbean Sea, many miles from the scene. Don't you think that seems a bit odd?"

The inspector made a good point. Why, at this time, and without informing anyone of his plans, had Darkside elected to take a vacation?

"All I can say is that I had nothing to do with the kidnap of my sheikh."

"Alright," said the inspector, looking at one of the guards. "That's all for now. We're going to keep you here for a few days, just as a precautionary measure."

"What for, what do you think I will do? If I had been a part of this terrible scheme, do you really believe I would come back here?"

"It's not important what I think. It's more important what I do. And for the moment, I am going to keep you in custody. I'm not saying you were involved, but if you were not, we will know very shortly. And then you will be released."

"Solamar, you know me," said Darkside. "I could never harm my sheikh. I have not been a part of this terrible thing.

You must believe me."

With a hardened look on his face, Solamar, the guard assigned to place Darkside in his cell, said, "I hope you have not, my friend. For your sake, I hope you have not."

Remembering his days behind bars in that filthy Turkish prison, an old empty feeling of helplessness wrapped around him like a cold wet blanket. Once again Darkside was alone, sitting with his head in his hands, his mind a swirl of disbelief. What had happened to his sheikh, what was happening to him, but most of all, what had Callie done to him?

Chapter 25

Johnny sat motionless in front of his word processor as the evening faded from dark to midnight. He knew he'd have to recount the thrills of the race, but he could not. Not until he finished his article about the foals. It read...

In my years on earth, I have had the good fortune to be in exactly the right place at exactly the right time on many a fine occasion. I have had the pleasure of meeting the Queen of England when she was here several years ago. I have interviewed presidents and met countless celebrities from all walks of life and from almost every country. But the most pleasant aspect of my life and the most exciting place my career ever takes me is to Churchill Downs the first Saturday in May. Yesterday, while I was in Louisville doing what I love most, I was plagued by a story running through my mind that I knew I would have to bring to the printed page today. Not about the Run for the Roses, or anything associated with the Derby at all, but a story about horses and the livelihood of those who depend on them.

Friday morning I witnessed a scene I will remember until the day I die: Horsemen, carrying foal fetuses and stillborn carcasses, lined up at the Kentucky Livestock and Diagnostic Center waiting patiently for an explanation as to what caused their prized mares to abort.

As I reported in 1996, following a plethora of stillborn foals, there is once again something causing many of the Thoroughbred mares in Central Kentucky to miscarry. Veterinarians in the area are reporting abnormal foalings with the placenta coming out first, as well as fully developed foals born listless, many of which die within hours.

The Kentucky Equine Research Center has prepared a survey to send to a vast majority of the horse farms in the

Central Kentucky area, and plans to analyze the data regarding the magnitude of the problem.

"This is a very serious problem," said Dr. Meredith Pehlagrem, an epidemiologist at the research center. The Kentucky Livestock and Diagnostic Center has begun performing necropsies to help determine the cause and has seen from 30 to 60 cases per day for the past week. Problems with other breeds of animals in Kentucky have not been reported, nor has there been a problem in the surrounding states. Needless to say, if the current trend continues, the future of Kentucky's Thoroughbred industry could well be in jeopardy.

Chapter 26

An Evening in Lexington

Tuck and Gwen sat in the corner of the Merrick Inn, gingerly swallowing a couple of Bud Lights as the waitress laid a platter of fried banana peppers on the table between them.

"Man, that looks good," said Gwen.

"How about two more Buds?"

After finishing their meal and a couple of shots of Woodford Reserve, Tuck's favorite bourbon, the once and future lovers drove over to Fairhaven Farm.

"Ya know I never get tired of driving out this road," said Tuck as the warm evening air filled the cab of the old Ford truck.

"Me neither. I miss this place."

"I never did know why you moved away when ya did. Guess I never will."

"Aw, Tuck, you know. I would have stayed, but..."

"Sure wish you hadn't moved away, Gwen."

"Yeah, I know. But you've got your farm and your horses and you know. And I've got my..."

"Your what? Career? And you can't have a career here in Kentucky? Hell, Gwen, they'd fight to get you back."

She remembered how it was five years ago when she packed up and left, mostly because Tuck had always seemed to be so busy with his work, and there never seemed to be enough time for the two of them. She remembered how she left without really giving him a chance to talk about it and that she drove down to Florida for the interview which she accepted right on the spot. She called Tuck and told him, just before leaving town. They'd stayed in touch over the years through the Internet, and he'd send her a card from time to time, but that was the extent of their relationship which had its flowering vine clipped just as the buds were beginning to blossom. She knew she'd hurt Tuck, but she also knew that she'd hurt herself. She didn't know how badly at the time, but the longer she was away from him, the more she longed to be back by his side.

"Do you want me to come back, Tuck?" The words were out of her mouth before she realized what she'd asked. In just one sentence, she'd summarized everything she'd been thinking for the past five years, dumping it in his lap.

Tuck looked at her and in a flash said, "Not only yeah, but hell, yeah."

Sensing that old protected feeling she'd experienced the first time he'd placed his arms around her, she allowed the warmth of the moment to overtake her resting her petite frame against the back of the pickup seat.

"You don't know how good you've just made me feel," she said.

"Well, I mean it, Gwen. I think you belong here in Kentucky."

Looking at him as he drove into the small parking lot next to the foaling barn, she continued gazing at him as the truck came to a stop. They sat suspended in time before he said, "And I think you belong with me."

"Oh, Tuck," she said, sliding over into his arms, "I love you." She felt almost giddy as she allowed her fears to float away.

"I love you, Gwen, I always have."

Chapter 27

"How are you feeling?" asked Anya as Efram emerged from his bath, dressed in the clothes she'd laid out for him.

"I do not know. I cannot tell just yet."

"Drink this. You will feel better," she said, handing him a mug of strong Turkish coffee.

"Now, do you like eggs? I can make you some eggs, and I have some cheese and some bread."

"Yes, thank you. That would be very good."

After several moments of silence, she handed him the plate of warm food and sat quietly looking at him while he ate.

"Do you know where you are?" she asked.

"No, I do not."

"You were brought here by an old friend of mine. How is it that you know him?"

"I do not know him. I am confused. I do not remember him."

"He told me that you are in danger and that there are men looking for you… looking to kill you. Is this true?"

"I know of no one looking to kill me. Where am I?"

"You are on a farm. We work the fields and live from the land."

"What farm?"

"You are in Turkey."

"Turkey? How did I get here?"

"My friend brought you."

"This friend of yours, did he say how it is I came to be in Turkey?"

"He told me that you are in trouble. That there are men who want to kill you. And," she hesitated, "that you are a, a sheikh."

"Can you help me?"

"What would you like me to do?"

Efram thought about her question for several moments before answering. "I have no memory of who I am. I do not know where I belong."

"Then you must rest. When the time is right, I will help you. You do not know of these men who want to kill you?"

"Why would they want to kill me?"

"I cannot answer what I do not know. The world is a mysterious place. I know only that you must proceed with caution."

"Who are you? What is your name?"

"I am Anya."

"Anya," he said slowly, allowing the handsome woman's name to reverberate through the confines of his soul. He sat motionless for a long moment before Anya asked, "And what is your name?"

"I, I do not know. I cannot remember."

"And do you expect me to believe that?" she asked, thinking that he was just trying to avoid the question.

"No," he said, smiling and taking a long drink from his coffee. "I do not. I cannot believe it myself. But it is true. As unbelievable as it may sound, it is true."

She thought for a moment before returning his smile and replying, "I believe you."

"If you help me, I will see that you are rewarded."

"How can you reward me? Are you really a sheikh? And anyway, what makes you think I want your money?"

Realizing that he may have offended her, he said, "I am not talking about money. If you or your people need anything, I will help you."

Something in the way he'd spoken, or the tone of his voice, pierced her heart.

"I can see that you are a man who thinks of others. There are not enough men in the world like that. You are rare."

She is right, he thought, as his long-term memory was

jogged, overriding his sketchy short-term memory. He always did think of others before thinking of himself. It was a trait he'd learned from his father who'd learned it from his father before him, one that, for whatever reason, had missed his brother, Rajad. Vaguely, yet instantly, streamed thoughts of his family and his past broached his mind. As Anya busied herself about the campsite he remembered how Rajad had always competed with him for the attentions of their father, refusing to understand that it was his selfishness as much as birth order that kept him in second place within the family hierarchy. Even though he never understood why Rajad had hated him, he tolerated and handled it well. Many times he and his father would talk about Rajad's shortcomings, but always lovingly and with prayers that Rajad would someday grow to become a man deserving of his heritage.

Thoughts of the infamous visit to his father's office trickled through his mind. On that sad and regrettable day, he'd been forced, by his duty to the welfare of the country, to bring news to his father that Rajad had grossly overrun his budget. Unknowingly, he'd set in motion the foreboding final scene. His long-term memory seemed to be intact as he remembered how he and Rajad had arrived at the main office building at precisely the same time. Rajad had begun accusing Efram of making him look bad and causing a rift between Rajad and their father. They'd been arguing for several moments outside the royal office when their father, overhearing them, came out pleading... "Please, my sons, let us not have this incessant bickering."

"Father, he is allowed so much more money for his hospitals and schools, and I am given a pittance of what he receives," complained Rajad in a heated voice.

"Do you really believe your horses and your equine facility are of the same value as our schools and hospitals? If I have led you to believe that, my son, I have done you a grave disservice."

As Efram sat motionless, he remembered, further, the final

incident. Their father knew that Rajad had labored hard to develop his dream but thought he was now acting selfishly. Efram, on the other hand, had neither political desires nor self-serving goals, and, even though both he and his father wanted Rajad to be successful, their priorities remained with the success of their people.

Trying to lighten the moment and avoid any further argument, Efram said, "Perhaps next year, when the budget is recalculated, we could,"

"To hell with your budget!" yelled Rajad, cutting him off in mid-sentence. "That is all I ever hear," he screamed, feeling that Efram was patronizing him, upstaging him in front of their father.

"Enough!" cried their father. "What must I do to stop this arguing? You must understand, Rajad, that we do not have unlimited funds for you to build everything you desire. You must rethink your needs and remain within your budget. These rules do not only apply to you. They apply to us all."

"All except Efram," said Rajad, bitterly.

"Rajad, my brother, a year will pass quickly. Maybe we can work together and complete your dream."

Of all the things Efram could have said at that precise moment, he picked the one that sent Rajad into a fury. Although he hated his brother, Rajad had never before disclosed his innermost feelings to his father, until now.

"You and I will do nothing together, you pilfering bastard." The words were out of his mouth before he'd realized what he'd said, and to whom.

"Rajad, you will not say that about your brother!" ordered the sheikh.

Realizing he'd gone too far, Rajad stood glaring at Efram without speaking.

"Do you hear me? I demand you answer me!"

With his face reddening and blood pressure on the rise their father was, for the first time in front of his sons, about to lose his temper.

Rajad searched for words to respond but knew he'd finally reached his limit. He had sinned, and in front of his father. He'd acted despicably and he knew it, but his rage and hatred were overwhelming.

"Rajad, I," said the patriarch, grabbing his chest and falling to the floor.

"Father!" cried Efram kneeling over him. "Go, get help," he ordered Rajad, but Rajad stood transfixed.

"Rajad, go get help!" he ordered a second time, "Rajad!"

Efram could hear his brother's name echoing through the sound-deadened halls of his mind. But even the death of their beloved father could not thwart his brother's hatred. Efram didn't know that it was this final act of perceived back-stabbing which convinced Rajad that, in order to survive and thrive within Karoumi's political infrastructure, he had to get rid of Efram. Rajad had contracted the Knights of the Caliphate to plant the bomb on Efram's plane that would allow Rajad to ascend the throne once his older brother was out of the way. His plan was thwarted when the bomb had been mistakenly taken off the plane. Efram didn't know all the details of the bomb, but was slowly realizing that Rajad had wanted him dead and had paid Kazeem and his Knights to do it.

Those were some rather strange, heart-breaking days which caused Efram to develop the stomach problems so exacerbated by the strong sedative he'd been given during his kidnapping.

But who were they? Why had they captured me? And why did they let me go? Thought Efram.

Unable to remember recent events, his mind turned back to Jules Weherner. He never knew that it was Jules who developed the genetic poison that Darkside brought to Kentucky. He was unaware that it was Jules who'd killed Rajad after he'd bullied and abused her.

It was all too confusing for Efram as he tried to make sense of the mesh of thoughts firing through his mind.

Apparently he was a sheikh, but a sheikh of what? Where was his homeland?

Waving her hand in front of his face, Anya tried to regain the pensive sheikh's attention. "Are you in there?" she asked. "Hello."

"I, I'm sorry. But thank you for saying that. It is true. I do not think of myself very often, that much I can recall."

"That is because you are used to thinking of others. You are different."

"I am not different than you. I am just a man that is all."

"I can see that you are not wearing a wedding ring. Are you married?"

Surprised at the nonchalant way she'd asked him, Efram thought for a moment, his memory a jumbled mass of reactions and impressions. After a long pause, he answered, "I was married, once. I loved her very much."

"Do you have children?"

"I have no children."

With a concerned look on her face, she said, "I believe you want children. Is that something you wish for?"

"I can not say. I did want children, but," He remained silent for a long moment.

"I believe you do. I know when people are not truthful, and you are not that way."

"Is that important to you, the truth?"

"Truth is always important to me. It is the foundation of our character. Who are we if not the truth? When we are untruthful, we plot against Allah."

"It is important to me also," said Efram, realizing that he'd been enjoying the conversation more than he'd enjoyed anything in a very long time. "I too am a student of Allah. I pray for his guidance in everything I do."

"Then what has brought you here? Who are you, and from where did you come?"

Dehydration, along with the neurological shock his system had endured from the anesthesia and kidnapping, left him with a limited paralysis of his temporal abilities. His memory was compromised. Realizing he was becoming uneasy, Anya thought that her questions might stimulate his memory.

"I do not know. I only wish I did, but I do not."

With tears welling in his eyes, he began piecing together minute details of a life that seemed held together like a loosely knit shawl. Seeing the distressed demeanor of her guest, Anya moved over to sit beside the pitiful-looking man, placing her arm around his shoulder to comfort him. And in this tender moment, they sat as two orphaned children, each offering the time-worn gift of comfort as only those who've suffered through the tragic loss of a precious loved one can do.

"I am sorry, I, I feel," whispered Efram, as he rested his head upon Anya's shoulder.

Sensing that it had been a long time since he'd allowed himself to express his inner emotions, she gently stroked the side of his head.

"Do not apologize to me," she said, running her fingers tenderly through his hair. "I understand. You are with me now. And I will take care of you. Do not worry."

They sat comfortably around the campfire until the sun had gone down and the coldness of the evening forced them inside. Efram slept soundly that night as thoughts of who he was and where he was going danced in and out of his mind.

I wonder what is next? He thought, drifting off to sleep. *Dear Allah, please tell me... what is next?*

Chapter 28

When Ramone and Stavrok arrived at the Chrixus and found the ship abandoned, they knew, immediately, they'd been double-crossed.

"Where is everyone?" yelled Stavrok.

"They are gone. But look at this," said Ramone, holding up the chain which had held Efram captive. "He has taken that sheikh with him."

"Why would he do that?"

"He plans to kill him somewhere else or wants more money. That is it. He wants more money. He knows they will pay more than ten-million dollars."

"But where have they gone?"

"That I do not know. He must have a place," said Ramone, searching his memory for a hideout where Kazeem would have gone.

"I will find him. And when I do," his eyes burned like coals as he twisted the chain around his fist, smashing it against the table.

"How will we find him?"

"We must contact that man who accompanies the sheikh's stable master. The one we paid to make sure he went on that vacation. What is his name?"

"I believe he is called Sela."

"Sela, he will know if Kazeem has demanded more money."

Late that night, a cell phone rang in a small town in Karoumi.

"Sela, this is Ramone. Are you going to remain in Karoumi?"

"Why do you call me? I know nothing. I do not want to be

involved."

"Listen to me. You are involved, very involved."

"I had nothing to do with this. I would never have done what I did if I thought you were going to kidnap my sheikh."

"You must do one more thing. You must find out if there has been a demand for more money."

"How can I do that? Why should I do that?"

"You must go to Beladesh and find that woman, that secretary."

"I do not know her."

"You must find out if the sheikh is alive and if there has been a demand for more money."

"The sheikh has not been found. I do know that. But why must I find out about the money?"

"Just do it. Or would you rather I call them myself and tell them about you?"

"I am not part of this. I want nothing to do with you or your gang."

"You did not mind taking the money we paid you to get that sheikh's friend out of the way."

Sela was no terrorist and knew nothing of the plot to kidnap the sheikh. All he'd known was that he would be rewarded handsomely if he solicited Callie to take Darkside on a vacation. He only facilitated the transaction; the money she received for her services was electronically transferred to her bank account. Although he should have known better, as far as Sela was concerned, he was only doing Darkside a favor.

"But that was only a vacation. I knew nothing about this, this plot to kidnap my sheikh."

"If you do this for us, my friend, you will never again hear from us. I only want to know if the sheikh is dead. And if there has been further demand for money. That is all."

"And if I do this, how can I be sure you will leave me alone?" asked a fearful Sela, realizing he'd become involved in a nightmare, one he wanted to go away.

"What else would we need from you? You will never hear

from us again, my friend."

"What do you want me to do?"

"I will contact you in two days. You should be able to find out the information by then. Tell no one."

"They will suspect something if I start asking questions."

"Go to see the secretary. Only talk to her. She will know, believe me. She will know. I will call you in two days."

"And then you will leave me alone? You will never again call me?"

"We will never again call you, Sela, my friend."

Sela breathed a sigh of relief. He'd known nothing of the plot to kidnap the sheikh but was not about to turn down a nice bit of money for what he thought would be a good time for Darkside. Having travelled with the stable manager for several years, he knew that Darkside was in need of some time off.

What have I done, thought Sela, pacing the floor of his small apartment. *I have betrayed my sheikh.*

Chapter 29

Callie spent the night on the seventh deck curled up with her bourbon bottle. She awoke late in the afternoon, somewhere between Barbados and San Juan, with an enormous hangover from bourbon and tears. She scoffed at the taste in her mouth lighting the first cigarette of her final day at sea. Stumbling back down four levels to her cabin, she opened one of the small water bottles she'd kept in the room taking an enormous swig.

Her thirst partially relieved, she sat on the edge of the bed, her head in her hands, allowing thoughts of the man who'd left her on the dock the day before to fill her conscience. In spite of the bourbon, she thought of very little else.

Where would he be right now? She thought. Looking at her watch, she realized that she'd been asleep for most of the day, and had missed, not only the breakfast call, but the luncheon as well.

Oh well, one more night and we'll be in San Juan. Ha! Who the hell are we? It's just you baby, just you.

She ordered her last meals from room service, not wanting to explain the sudden disappearance of the man who'd accompanied her. The final morning, she left the ship and spent the better part of the morning getting to the airport in San Juan. Following a long delay checking in, it was finally her turn at the counter when she heard...

"Excuse me, miss," said a tall man in casual dress. "Would you please come with me?"

"What's this about?" asked Callie.

Following the man to a small office, she was asked about her relationship with Wanda Groselli.

"I haven't seen her in years," said Callie.

"You had no idea that she was on the ship that you have just left?" asked the detective.

"No, I did not. What's this all about? Is she in some kind of trouble?"

"There was a murder on board. We saw the security video of your friend's cabin-mate being thrown off the deck."

Callie's blood ran cold, but her cat-like senses kicked in. "What makes you think I know anything about that? I didn't even know she was alive, much less on the ship."

"They all got off the ship and never came back. And the man you were with got off the ship and never came back. We know that you used to work with Ms. Groselli," said the detective. "Why wouldn't we think that you had something to do with it?"

"How did you know that we'd worked together? I mean where did you get that information?"

The detective did not respond immediately but shuffled some papers on his desk before saying without looking up, "Information is what I do."

"I haven't seen Wanda Groselli in years. I told you that."

"Now why should I believe you?" he asked coldly. "Is this just a bizarre coincidence? You knew her, you are on the same ship, and your partner gets off before completing the trip. A man is coincidentally thrown overboard by your former friend, and they get off the ship before completing the trip. Do you expect me to believe you knew nothing about this?"

"I expect you to believe the truth," said Callie.

"Yes, of course. I know you don't mind remaining with us until we sort this out, do you?"

"The hell I don't! Are you arresting me?" demanded Callie.

"We have the right to hold you."

"The hell you do! Arrest me if you must, but if you're not gonna do that, then leave me alone," she yelled, scrambling out of the office.

She quickly lost herself in the crowd, certain they would follow. Surprisingly, she was not approached as she made her way to her gate boarding her plane. Following an arduously long and painful flight through Atlanta to Lexington, it hit her like a wave as she rode alone in the backseat of the taxi.

What am I doing in Lexington without him? I must go find him. He'll need me, and I need him. I must go.

She paid the fare and carried her luggage into the house. Retrieving her mail, she barely glanced at the bills before reaching for the phone book.

"Delta Airlines, may I help you?"

"Yes, I would like a one-way ticket to the United Arab Emirates."

"Yes, ma'am, would that be to Dubai?" asked the cheerful voice of the ticket agent with a southern accent.

"No, Karoumi. I need to go to Karoumi."

"Certainly, ma'am, I can route you through, well, you still must go through Dubai and then into Karoumi aboard Emirates Express."

"Whatever, I just need to go as soon as possible."

"And where will you be departing?"

"Lexington, Kentucky."

"Alright, ma'am I can do that for you. You can depart tomorrow morning at 11:30 a.m. from Lexington to New York. From there you'll fly aboard Emirates Airlines departing JFK, arriving in Dubai at 8:30 a.m. the following day. From Dubai, you catch the Emirates Express shuttle on into Karoumi. How does that sound?"

"Sounds like I better take a good book with me."

Callie finished the transaction, mixed herself a highball, and threw her suitcase onto the bed in anticipation of repacking. She needed to get organized since she had only hours before heading back to the airport to continue the most significant adventure of her life.

Even though the ride out over the Atlantic was smooth and uneventful, she could not find the comfort zone necessary to afford her the sleep she so desperately craved. Every time she was just about to doze off, thoughts of Darkside overtook her tired mind.

She tried watching the on-board movie but couldn't concentrate long enough to keep up with the story. With all the things she was thinking about, she wished she had someone to talk to. It dawned on her that she had so very few friends, and the few she did have had been men. She didn't really know what it was about the females, but there was always something she distrusted in them.

For all of her seeming disdain, Callie preferred men. She understood what motivated them and enjoyed their money and the power she had over them. Some were interesting, and she'd always liked interesting people. Endless chat about clothes, hair, makeup, and fingernails bored her to tears. Then she married Herman.

Herman, she thought, *you sure didn't set the world on fire, but you were safe. I'll give you that. You were safe. And I did love you.*

But just why did she marry Herman when she did? Was it the money? She knew, no matter how she tried to rationalize it, the money was definitely a factor. She enjoyed having the things she'd always dreamed about, but most of all she liked the prestige that went along with being his wife. He was such a powerful man. Not so much with regard to his physical abilities, but more so in his character. With her flamboyant lifestyle before she met him, she had to admit that her years with Herman were the best days of her life.

"Excuse me, ma'am, would you like something to drink?" asked the cheerful stewardess.

"Yes, I'll have bourbon?"

"There you go; that will be ten dollars."

Callie poured both bottles into the plastic cup of ice the stewardess had given her, topping it off with a smidgen of water. She took several long sips before continuing her memories.

Here's to you, Herman, she thought, toasting her former husband. *You were always good to me. I don't think I ever told you that, but you were. And I loved you. I really did.*

Finishing the strong drink, she stumbled out of her seat and back to the galley where she purchased two more of the little bottles. Mixing a second drink, she began sipping it just as the airplane encountered turbulence.

"Ladies and gentlemen, the captain has turned on the seat belt light indicating that we may encounter some rough air. For your own protection, we kindly ask you to return to your seats and fasten your seat belts. Thank you."

Shit, let it rain, let it pour, let the whole damn world fade away, she thought looking out her window into the black ocean heaving 34,000 feet below. She very seldom held, what she and the other girls at Pauline's called, a pity party, but she felt in the mood to sulk, at least for the next 3,000 miles.

She showed every minute of her 30 plus hours with no sleep stepping out of the small twin-engine Brazilia shuttle plane Emirates Express used for the 20 minute ride from Dubai to Beladesh. Unable to speak the language and not knowing anyone except Darkside, she made her way into the airport coffee-shop and ordered a bottle of lime-flavored water.

Recovering her belongings from the luggage carousel, she walked outside the terminal where she found a cab waiting to take her to the Crown Plaza, the new and ornate, oil-rich hotel she'd seen advertised on the airport walls. Once in her room, she undressed, poured two fingers of bourbon from the bottle she'd stowed in her suitcase, and slipped into a tub of hot, steamy bubbles. Realizing she didn't know exactly where to start her search, she began to relax as the warmth of the bath and the serenity of the opulent surroundings soothed her.

Now, she thought, *all I have to do is find him.*

Chapter 30

"Alright people," said Dr. Meredith Pehlagrem, trying to bring order to the vast array of doctors and scientists gathered in the large auditorium-like classroom at the Diagnostic Center. "Let's try to get started. It..." she stopped momentarily, allowing the conversation in the room to die down.

"It appears that we are dealing with a problem which is growing substantially worse every day. Since we have so many folks coming to our aid, we think it best if we divide and conquer. Many of you know Doctor Gardot who was instrumental in solving the problem of foal-deaths in '96. She has graciously offered her services and has driven up from Florida to be with us once again."

"Excuse me, Doctor, but was there a definitive solution found for the problems of 1996?" asked a toxicology expert who'd flown in that morning from Illinois.

"We were able to determine that those particular foal-deaths were all from a very select group of stallions, and, therefore, we were able to quarantine all affected animals. But to answer your question, Doctor, no, we were not able to determine an exact source or a definitive solution for the problems then."

With the room in a stir, Dr. Pehlagrem began again.

"I would like to, first of all, divide into teams. Most of you know which team you will be assigned to, so I'm hoping we won't have to waste time getting started. Maybe then we can gain some momentum. We feel that five teams should be appropriate, but nothing is chiseled in stone, so please feel free to make any suggestions. The first team will consist of the toxicological group, those who will be taking pasture samples and performing the associated clinical testing. The second group is the reproductive study group. The Jockey Club has offered to assist us with researching bloodlines and breeding records. Third, will be the epidemiological people. You folks will be performing the animal comparisons. Fourth, are the financial people whose job it will be to find the funding which will offset some of the costs of all the testing. And fifth, the communications group. I will be a member of this bunch, and will be serving as overall liaison. One thing I do want to cover is how we handle the press."

All eyes were glued on Meredith as she looked at each person in the room.

"We will be working some very long hours. You must know how terrible this problem is to the horsemen whose farms we will visit. Please be cognizant of your attitude and behavior when confronted by these folks, and especially when talking to the press. This may be the most important work of your career, and you never know how the equine community will react. My only suggestion to you is to place yourself in their shoes. They are losing millions of dollars and many of them may well be bankrupt as a result. Practice patience, and be as kind and as informative as you can. I think it would be wise not to discuss any details with anyone until we have had a chance to get together and report to the media with one voice.

If members of the media approach you directly, ask them to call me and give them my phone number. I will handle the press from here. I also think we should have a disclosure meeting within a couple of days where we can provide the community with an update of our progress. I will pull that together, and I think we should all be prepared to speak at that time and disclose what we have. If we don't know anything by then, that's exactly what we'll say.

We have prepared a list of teams and associated people, so if you feel you are on the wrong team, now is the time to speak up. We have included the phone numbers of those of us who will remain here at the center and numbers of farm managers and equine specialists around the community. I will update this list frequently, so if you need updates I will get them to you. Most of you have portable fax machines, so there shouldn't be a problem. Let me just conclude with one reminder. We have babies dying. We must find and cure what's killing them. And I just want to say..." Meredith paused briefly. "I, I just want to thank you. Thank you all from the bottom of my heart."

When the room emptied, Meredith asked Gwen when they could expect the results from the questionnaire, which had been sent to over 100 farms in the Central Kentucky area.

"I'd say we should see some coming back as early as tomorrow. That's when I plan to begin normalizing the data."

"My secretary can help you with that. She's a whiz at data entry and querying that database she's set up."

"Great. I'll touch base with her just as soon as I finish here."

"Anything you need, just ask," said Meredith.

"Doctor Pehlagrem, there is one thing I would like to ask you."

"What happened to Bill and me?"

"I'm sorry, Doctor, I shouldn't pry. I just remember you and Bill were, so close."

"We were close; we were very close. But," she hesitated, trying to find just the right words. "It's just that once we settled here in Lexington, he didn't want to rush back into a life-long commitment so soon after his divorce. So after a time we just drifted apart, and he went back to Virginia and reopened his clinic."

"I am sorry, Doctor. I truly am," said Gwen as her cell phone started ringing.

"I know, dear, and I appreciate your concern."

"Hello, this is Gwen."

"And this is Tuck."

"Hi, and just how's my favorite man?"

"Wanting some more of your company, any chance I can see you tonight?"

"When can you be here?"

"Seven seemed to work the last time; how's that sound?"

"I'll be ready."

Tuck picked her up in exactly the same place as the day before, but this time he drove straight to Fairhaven Farm, where he'd taken time that afternoon to clean and air out his room in the back of the foaling barn. After an evening of wine, cheese, Italian bread, and the most satisfying love-making either of them had experienced in years, the couple lay quietly on the small antique bed, wrapped tightly in each other's arms.

"Oh my," said Gwen. "Ask me if I'm happy."

"Are you happy?"

"Mmmmm, I feel like the cat that ate the canary."

"I'll be your canary, anytime."

"Can we stay this way forever?"

"I don't see why not. Provided you come back to Kentucky?"

"Do you really want me to come back, Tuck?"

"Now what do you think? What the hell ever made you think I wanted you to leave in the first place?"

"I don't know, but you know how busy you always are. I mean with the horses and all. And I'm not complaining, I know how much it takes to do your job. I know that."

"And what about your job, it don't take time to do that? Of course it does. It's just that, life is so empty without you, Gwen, and so damn full with you in it."

Tuck had said the right thing to the right person at just the right time, as Gwen looked deep into his eyes.

"What if I do come back? What then?"

"Well, I don't know, maybe we could get married or something'."

"Are you serious?"

"Yes I am."

"Oh my," said Gwen, "oh my."

Chapter 31

Darkside sat in his cell trying not to think about the days aboard the Matriarch and the temptress who'd robbed him of his liberty. No matter how much he hated what she'd done to him, he knew that he had no one to blame but himself. Even though he tried his best to keep her out of his mind, he could not. He could not stop the constant flood of thoughts of her laughter and their lovemaking. He could not, he sadly realized, hold back the sea.

"Mr. Prahstomank," said Inspector Edwards, "there is a lady here to see you. She claims that you were with her on a cruise to the Caribbean, and that she was paid a lot of money to take you on a vacation."

Darkside remained silent.

Edwards continued, "She flew in yesterday and she's here now. I say, this may give your story credence after all."

"Did she say that we were on the Matriarch of the Seas? And that we flew to San Juan?"

"As a matter of fact, she did. We verified it with the cruise line. I'm going to release you on one condition."

"And what is that?"

"That you, under no circumstances, try to leave the country."

"What about my sheikh?"

"We still don't know about the sheikh. We have not heard from him, nor do we know whether he's..." the detective did not complete the sentence.

"I must find my sheikh. You do not understand. I must find my sheikh!" shouted Darkside.

"Now look here, I'll tell you what you must and musn't do. And what you better not do is leave the country."

Realizing that he was in no position to argue, Darkside simply nodded his head accepting the conditions set forth by the inspector.

"I will not attempt to leave the country."

"Good, then. By the way, that lady seems to care an awful lot about you. I think you owe her a debt of gratitude. She was quite upset when she learned that we were keeping you in custody and quite insistent that we free you at once."

"She should be!" barked Darkside in a stern, bitter tone.

"Quite a lady indeed," responded Inspector Edwards.

"I do not wish to see her," said Darkside.

"And what would you have me tell her?"

"Forgive me, Inspector, but that is up to you. I just know that I do not wish to see her."

"Well have it your way, but if I were you I'd at least thank her for getting you out of jail."

"Another time, perhaps but, not now."

Darkside returned to the sanctity of his apartment to collect his thoughts and plan his strategy. He'd learned from Callie, during her confession while on-board the Matriarch, that it was Sela who'd solicited her to take him on the cruise, which led him to believe that Sela was directly responsible for the disappearance of the sheikh. Knowing the town where Sela was born, he prepared to track down the back-stabbing traitor when he was interrupted by a knock on his door.

"Enter, it is open."

Darkside had not expected to see the enemy, Sela, at his door.

"I, I," said Sela, fighting back tears. "I do not know what to say to you, Sasha." Falling to his knees, he remained prostrate in front of his boss.

Trying hard to maintain his emotions, Darkside asked, "And what am I to say to you, Sela?"

"Please, Sasha, please believe me I, I had no idea. I only wanted you to be happy on your vacation. The lady told me that she would take good care of you. I wanted you to be happy. You work so hard."

"And what of our sheikh, who is taking care of him?"

"I knew nothing of the sheikh. You must believe me I knew nothing about what happened to him. I would never hurt our sheikh, never!"

"How can I believe you? You have disgraced us all."

"I know you cannot forgive me. I know that. I only ask that you believe that I had nothing to do with the sheikh. I would never harm our sheikh. Please, you must know that," he sobbed, his voice cracking.

Whether it was the way his body shook uncontrollably or the tone in his tear-drenched dialogue, something penetrated Darkside enough causing him to place his arms around the small man. A man who had, until the sheikh's abduction, been his closest, and most constant companion. He knew Sela well enough to know that he was telling the truth.

"It is alright. I believe you. I do."

Sela raised himself from the floor and fell into Darkside's arms, hugging him tightly. After several anguishing moments, Darkside listened to him tell everything he knew.

"This Ramone, he will call you tomorrow night?"

"Yes. I am to find out if there has been a further demand for money."

"And he did not know the whereabouts of the sheikh?"

"No, he said that he thought he might be dead, but he did not know. That is why he believes there will be a demand for more money."

"Something must have gone wrong with their plot. They must have missed the money drop, or there was a double-cross. Who, if not him, would be in a position to demand more money? Their group has become divided."

Darkside's eyes sparkled, thinking for the first time that the sheikh may still be alive.

"Where is Ramone?"

"That I do not know. I know that they are all from Turkey. They call themselves the Knights of the Caliphate."

The name struck a chord within Darkside's heart, as memories of the filthy Turkish prison exploded in his mind.

"We will await Ramone's call together. I will tell you what to say. I am beginning to smell something foul in the air. Now, I must go out for a while, but I will return. Remain here, I will be back soon. We will receive his call together."

Chapter 32

The coolness of the morning painted Beladesh with a much-needed reprieve after several days of unseasonably hot weather. Seeing Darkside and Sela walk through the office door, Najema ran from her desk and into the arms of one of Karoumi's favorite sons.

"Thank Allah, you are out," she rejoiced.

Hugging her tightly, Darkside asked, "Have you heard from him?"

Najema's expression quickly changed to a frown as she shook her head no.

"Sasha, I must tell you. The man I was seeing, Ab. He was a part of the kidnap."

"What do you remember of that day?"

"I do not remember much of anything. I have been confused since that day. The drug they gave me made me very sick. I was in the hospital for two days. Since then, I cannot recall what has happened. I am sorry, Sasha, I cannot."

"It is alright. No one is blaming you. You had no part in this. Allah knows that."

"I cannot believe they have taken my sheikh, right from this office. And I could not stop it."

"I am thankful that you are alive, has there been a demand for more money?"

"Why?"

"We believe that there has been a double-cross, and that they want more money. Has anyone called?"

"Inspector Edwards asked me to act as though nothing has happened. If there is a call, I should just take it and act naturally. But I have received no call. Not here."

Darkside suspected that Interpol would have had the

phone lines tapped and that any call for additional money would have been intercepted by Inspector Edwards.

"Good, that is all I need to know. I will be back to see you later. Right now, I want to talk with Inspector Edwards."

Darkside went, immediately to visit Inspector Edwards, who confirmed their suspicions.

"If there is a call, it's for us to deal with, not you," said the inspector in his customary matter-of-fact tone.

"I understand that, sir. I only ask if you have received such a call?"

"Well, no. I can say that there has been no call placed regarding demands for additional money, if that's what you're after. Why do you ask?"

"We have not heard of the whereabouts of our sheikh. We do not know what has happened to him."

"Let me set you straight about this once and for all. The sooner you get used to the idea that your sheikh is already dead, the better off you people will be. These terrorists don't leave a live trail."

Darkside glared as he fought to remain calm and not lose his temper.

"I will never accept that he is dead, NEVER!"

Darkside stormed out of the municipal building en route to his apartment to solidify plans to trap Ramone. He thought if he could lure Ramone into thinking that Karoumi would pay additional money, they could capture him and make him disclose the sheikh's whereabouts.

At nine o'clock that evening, Sela's cell phone rang and a familiar, ugly voice came over the line.

"Alright, my friend what can you tell me?" asked Ramone.

"There has been a demand of an additional ten-million dollars," said Sela.

"I knew it. And where is this to take place?"

"On the island of Buyukada."

"When?"

"It is as before. At five o'clock local time, just after the last ferry departs the island."

"And exactly where is the exchange to take place?" asked Ramone.

"In the middle of the village square, I believe it will be in a horse cart."

"And who will deliver the money?"

"That I do not know. All I do know is that at five o'clock, he must be at the center of town, and the money will be in a suitcase."

Ramone knew that it was a good plan and that it sounded like something Kazeem would concoct. Buyukada, a small island within an hour's ferry ride of Istanbul, would be perfect for such an exchange. The fact that there are no cars allowed on the island, and that most tourists would return Istanbul aboard the five o'clock ferry, placed the drop point in a perfect place. If Ramone knew Kazeem, he knew that there would also be an escape boat anchored somewhere close by. All he had to do was be in Buyukada before five o'clock and intercept the drop.

"That is good work, my friend," said Ramone. "You have done well for me. Have you heard anything about the welfare of your sheikh?"

"We have heard nothing. Do you know where he is?"

"That I do not know. Goodbye, my friend," said Ramone as the line went dead.

"So we have baited the trap. And now we must collect our prey. Like the noble falcon, perched on the hand of his master, we must attack our victim with the swiftness of the Peregrine and drink his blood with the victory of our kill."

Darkside knew what he was talking about, having accompanied Karoumi's chief falconer on many a hunting expedition. Riding out on their fabulous horses, dressed in robes of flowing white with the regal birds perched upon their leather gloves, was a noble and sacred sight to behold. In much the same way as their ancestors had done, they'd release their winged charges to stalk the small animal life of the desert.

True to traditional Bedouin custom, it is believed that the nomadic peoples of the Asiatic plains have practiced falconry for more than 2,000 years, as a means of augmenting their meager diet of milk, bread, and dates. Always ready to test the best Karoumi had to offer, Darkside would jump at the chance to retrace his heritage-laden steps. But it was now time to take the game to newer and loftier heights as he thought about how he could leave the country without causing a stir.

Should I tell Inspector Edwards of my plan? He thought. *Or just get in the plane and go? If I tell him, he might try to stop me, or worse, jeopardize the whole thing and endanger the sheikh. If I do not tell him, what will happen? I might go to jail. But what have I done wrong? Nothing! That is it, then. Since I have done nothing wrong and have committed no crime, I have nothing to fear by trying to save my sheikh.*

"It is settled then. We will fly to Turkey," said Darkside, as Sela's eyes brightened.

Chapter 33

It was a cold, rainy morning as Anya stirred the hot cereal she'd made for Efram's breakfast. The wind blew hard against the tied-down flaps of the old canvas tent as frigid drops of frozen sleet squeezed their way into the confines of the dilapidated domicile. The only brightening aspects of the environment were the cheerfulness with which Anya went about her task and the gentle ease Efram provided through nothing more than his presence.

"Good morning. And how is my sheikh today?" asked Anya, in her usual friendly manner.

"I have slept well. And I am hungry."

"I have breakfast for you and some hot coffee."

"Thank you, Anya. You are a true blessing."

Realizing that she hadn't had the opportunity to blush in such a long time, she allowed a broad smile to overtake her face.

"So how is your memory this morning?"

"I must try and find my way home. I know that."

"What is your hurry? Do you not like it here?"

"Oh, no, it has nothing to do with what I like. I must."

"I understand. I am only teasing you. Of course, you must find your home. And I will help you."

"And how is it that you think you can help me?"

"My brother will help."

"Are you not afraid of being caught?"

"I do not believe they are still looking for me. Besides, my brother will help us, I mean you."

She blushed a second time, realizing that she'd included herself in his quest, like they were partners. Failing to notice her remark, Efram continued to inquire about her safety. It had been nearly two weeks since he'd been taken from his home and over a week since he'd come to the campsite. He'd grown fond of the lady with whom he'd taken refuge. Over the course of the last eight days, Anya told Efram of her past, concluding with her unfortunate love affair with Kazeem.

"I would not want you to be in danger. That is foremost among my concerns," said Efram.

"I can take care of myself. But thank you for thinking of me. That is what I like about you. You always seem to be concerned with the welfare of others."

"And how do you know that? Do you think you know me?"

"I know you. I have been paying attention to what you have been saying these last few days. You do not speak of yourself."

"Is that such a bad thing?"

"Of course not, I like it. And I like you."

"What about your brother? What could he do for me?"

"That I do not know. But I do know that staying here is doing nothing. If you must find out who you are and where you belong, you must leave here. No?"

Efram nodded.

"Good. Then tomorrow, we go."

"And just how do we do that?"

"We can take the bus to Istanbul. I know where we can catch it and not draw attention."

"Do you have money for the bus?"

"I have some money. We will be fine."

"I will repay you when I..." Efram felt a flash of memory cross his mind.

"What is it?"

"I just saw myself in white robes, in an office, behind a desk."

"Then maybe you truly are a sheikh. Ah?"

Efram sat motionless, trying to make sense out of the jumbled mess of thoughts and memories shooting through his mind.

"Eat," ordered Anya, feeling somewhat miffed that his

attentions had drifted from her and their conversation.

"I am sorry. I just..."

They spent the remainder of the day in quiet discussion of their upcoming expedition while the wind blew the chilly rain in and about their humble abode. As the sun set, Efram warmed himself by the sweetness of Anya's smile.

Chapter 34

Darkside packed the handguns and placed several ammunition clips, along with a change of clothing into his duffle-bag.

"Did you bring the suitcase?" he asked, as Sela came through the apartment door. They were due at the airport, where the pilot was preparing the jet which would take them to their illicit rendezvous.

"Yes. And I have my clothes and some fruit. That is all."

"Here, you will need this," said Darkside, handing him a handgun.

"I know nothing of guns."

"There is nothing to it. I will show you when we get on the plane. Just make sure it is not loaded."

"How do I do that?"

Darkside smiled and pushed the release mechanism discharging the ammo clip. Opening the chamber, he removed the shell that remained in firing position before returning the gun to Sela.

"Now, it is unloaded. We will load it when we are ready to leave the plane."

"Do you think we will really need these?"

"Sela, look at me. These are murderers. They will kill you if they have to. I just hope that we can save the sheikh. Think only of the safety of the sheikh, and you will fare much better, my friend."

The Hawker 800 engines came alive as they made their way aboard the eight-passenger plane.

"Everybody ready?" asked the pilot, before taxiing out to the runway.

"We can only hope," answered Darkside buckling his

seatbelt.

"Say, what's the latest on the sheikh?"

"We have heard nothing. But we are hopeful, ah?"

The shimmering lights of Beladesh flew by as the small but nimble jet roared down the two-mile runway flinging itself into the hazy arms of the cool Arabian sky. The flight passed uneventfully as Darkside, having had little rest the last several days, fell into a blissful sleep. Following their landing at Yesilkoy Airport, they took a cab to the Galata Bridge, where they purchased tickets for the ferryboat that would take them to Buyukada.

"There will be a boat," said Darkside. "I know that he will have a boat. That is how he will make his escape. I will be carrying the suitcase, and you will keep me in your field glasses at all times. You are my backup. When we get to the island, we must leave the ferry separately. I will walk slowly toward the center of the square and go directly to the drop point. He will probably be riding a bicycle or a horse."

"How do you know that?" asked Sela.

"There are no motorized vehicles allowed on Buyukada. And I do not think that he will be on foot. That is too risky. There are many horses on the island. He will probably be on horseback."

"Where should I be?"

"You will be in the mass of people crowded at the gate and will get off as soon as the ferry docks. That way, if he is watching the boat, he will not see you. I do not know if he knows what I look like, but we cannot take that chance. I will wait and be the last one off. If he is watching, he will remain focused on me. I will stand in plain sight on the top deck. You will sneak off the boat while he is watching me."

It was just past four o'clock as the ferryboat's stern came to rest against the dock at Buyukada. Darkside stood on the upper deck, near the front wearing the red ball cap that Ramone had ordered. Sela, managed to slip off unseen.

The long blast from the whistle signaled to those on the

island that the last ferry back to Istanbul was arriving. Darkside's sweaty palm clasped the handle of the suitcase as he made his way down the steps and over to the gangway. Leaving the boat, he walked straight up into the main square of town. Seeing several horse-carts, he lifted the suitcase into the one closest to him, handing the driver a 50 lira bill. Sitting in the open cart, he looked around nervously while he tried to explain that he did not want to go anywhere, but that he was waiting for a friend. Not wanting to just sit and wait, the driver protested. Darkside handed him a second 50 lira bill. As their discussion grew to take on all the elements of an argument, no one noticed the horse-cart moving slowly down the street carrying the olive-skinned man dressed like one of the native Turkish inhabitants.

"Is that suitcase for me?" asked Ramone, as the cart in which he was riding pulled up. Darkside sat motionless as he turned to look into Ramone's eyes.

"Please, my friend, hand it to me," said Ramone.

"Where is my sheikh?" demanded Darkside.

"I do not know about your sheikh. I told you that already."

"Then why should I give you this money? If you cannot produce my sheikh, what am I paying for?"

"Do not be foolish; I have a gun. If you do not hand me the suitcase, I will be forced to shoot you."

Darkside stood up in the cart throwing the suitcase at Ramone, hitting him in the shoulder. Jumping into Ramone's cart, he stuck his pistol into the ribs of the unholy kidnapper, but the driver, seeing the gun, let out a harrowing yell, causing the horse to lurch forward. As they struggled, the startled horse raced down the street through throngs of tourists. The afternoon quiet was broken by the sound a single shot.

Seeing the horse-cart lurch forward, Sela chased after his friend with hopes of capturing Ramone, but his heart sank, as he saw his friend's body tossed out onto the street in front of him.

"Sasha!" cried Sela, racing to his side. "Sasha!"

But the fates had plotted against them as he fell onto the limp body of his mentor and compatriot. Having taken the bullet in the side of his body, Darkside lay unconscious.

When the emergency wagon arrived, they placed Darkside in the cart and raced to the local infirmary. When the on-call nurse saw the extent of the wound, she ordered an immediate transfer to Istanbul's Central Hospital. Not knowing what to do, Sela waited in the hallway, trying his best to answer questions the local constable fired at him.

Having made a clean getaway in his stolen runabout, Ramone didn't realize that he'd escaped with a suitcase full of rags. When he discovered he'd been outwitted, he vowed before Allah that he would enact his revenge.

"You will pay for this," he yelled, holding up his fist. "One day, I promise you. You will pay dearly for this."

Chapter 35

The Keeneland sales pavilion came to life at five o'clock, as more than 1,000 of Kentucky's equine society came together to hear Dr. Pehlagrem and the staff of scientists and doctors present their data to the overwrought, haggard crowd. Across the elevated platform sat a panel of 12 of the best minds in the equine industry. As each of the experts rose to give an update of her or his findings, Johnny Stone held his small recording device while scribbling in his notebook. From mycotoxins in the grass to the unseasonably warm spring weather, the doctors spoke for over two hours while Johnny sat spellbound.

Leaving the pavilion, he felt sad. What hit him the hardest was that they had their theories but had reported nothing solid; they still didn't know exactly what was killing the foals. He didn't fault their efforts; how could he? They'd been working around the clock since the ordeal began. What he couldn't believe was that they couldn't bring the issue to closure.

I certainly can't write that, he thought. *Give it time, Johnny, he kept telling himself. Give it time.*

Following the meeting, Tuck walked up to the platform where the scientists were gathered. Finding Gwen talking with one of the many television reporters, he smiled at her. Finishing her conversation, she moved quickly to his side.

"I spoke with Doctor Pehlagrem this morning," said Gwen.

"Oh?"

"She said I could come to work for her any time I wanted."

"Did she go into detail? I mean about what you would do and all that?"

"It didn't really seem that important. She said with my experience, I could do just about anything."

"That's great, Gwen. Great."

"Yeah, and I could come to work immediately."

"Did you tell her about us?"

"I didn't have to, she seemed to already know. She's quite a lady."

"So, what's next?"

"I'll have to go back to Florida and submit my resignation. Then pack my stuff and move back."

"Well, just as soon as we fix this little problem we're having here, we'll do just that," said Tuck.

Chapter 36

The rain had stopped and the sun was shining, as the vehicle that would take them to Istanbul stopped for the two raggedly dressed vagabonds to step hurriedly aboard. Paying the driver, they found their way to the back of the bus and began talking about their next encounter.

"What will you say to your brother?" asked Efram. "How will you approach him?"

"I will just call him up and say hello."

"I do not think that is the proper way to do this. I believe we should go directly to his home. Confront him there."

"Why do you say that?"

"Because I do not believe that you should give him time to think? We should just show up, and then he will not have an opportunity to be negative."

"But he is my brother. Why should he be negative? He will be happy to see me. Or at least he should be."

"You are correct; he should be. But how often do we act as we should?"

"But he is my brother," responded Anya.

"I had a brother once. He tried to kill me."

"No! Are you serious?"

"That is what I have been told. He tried to have me killed by blowing up a plane on which I was to travel."

"Why would your own brother want to kill you?"

"That, I will never know. But sometimes we do not act as we should. That I do know."

"So you think we should go directly to his house and just show up?"

"That is what I would do. Yes."

They sat quietly watching the countryside pass by the

filthy window of the mud-caked Mercedes-Benz bus. Arriving in Istanbul, they stopped long enough to secure her brother's address before grabbing a cab. Once in front of the apartment building, they entered the ornately decorated, up-scale complex.

"Your brother has done well," said Efram.

"He has connections. My father was a diplomat. I am sure he has been instrumental in the success of his only son."

"Are you his only daughter?"

"Yes, but I do not consider myself his daughter anymore. Or should I say that he does not consider me to be his."

"How long has it been since you have seen him?"

"I do not remember, many, many years ago. After I went into hiding, he disowned me."

"But you are his flesh and blood," said Efram.

"I disgraced him, and the family."

"What about your brother? Will he feel that way about you?"

"I believe," said Anya, raising her eyebrows, "that we are about to find out."

"What is his name?"

"Emil."

Arriving at Emil's apartment, Anya hesitated, momentarily, before knocking.

"Well, here goes."

"Wait, we should pray, Dear Allah," began Efram, "please help us. Please bring this brother and sister together within your graces, and heal the hurt from days gone by." With that, he knocked on the door.

"Yes," came the response as the door partially opened.

"I am looking for Emil Kozakaris," said Anya.

"I am Emil Koza..." said the soft-spoken father of two, stopping mid-sentence, realizing that he was looking into the eyes of his long, lost sister.

"Oh my, oh, my," he said, placing his hand over his mouth. "Am I seeing things?"

"Emil?" said Anya, bursting into tears.

"Anya," cried the tall, slightly overweight man, gathering his sibling into his arms.

After several moments of hugging and kissing, she turned saying, "Emil, this is a friend of mine who needs your help."

When Emil looked at Efram, his eyes widened and he gasped, "I know you. You have been on the TV. You have been kidnapped. You are the sheikh who has been kidnapped from the United Arab Emirates. It has been on CNN all week."

"So it is true. You ARE a sheikh," said Anya.

"I have been kidnapped?" asked Efram in disbelief.

"Yes, it has been on CNN for over a week now. Tell me, Anya," his smile changing to a frown, "how is it that you are involved in a kidnapping?"

"No," she laughed. "I am not involved with a kidnapping. He was brought to my campsite, and I am helping him return to his country."

Although happy to see his sister, Emil looked at her skeptically as thoughts of her illegal activities crossed his mind.

"Can you help us, Emil? We need help returning him to his home. That is all."

"And what about you, are you with him?"

Emil had asked the perfect question, one that neither could readily answer.

"Let us just say that he needs help and that I am his friend."

"Come inside; you must be famished. I would like you to meet my family."

Following introductions and a huge meal that Emil's wife Catryna cooked, Efram and Anya spent a relaxed evening, sipping tea and exchanging stories of Anya's youth. Emil seemed completely captured by the tales of his older sister, much to the chagrin of Catryna. With no desire to join in the discussion, her eyes reflected a growing disdain for her husband's sister. Unable to prevent the woman from dominating the conversation under her own roof, nor the interest shown to her by her husband, Catryna kept to herself, watching the unwelcome Gypsy behind wickedly silent black eyes. She had always despised Anya and the Knights of the Caliphate and knew about her rebellious escapades long before she and Emil had gotten married. She hated the kindness he was now affording his sister after stating many times that he would never speak to her again. It was nearing midnight before Emil turned on the television.

"Look," said Efram jumping to his feet. "I know him, I know him."

With news of the day's shooting at the island of Buyukada, an amateur's recording of Sela accompanying Darkside on a stretcher, flashed across the screen.

"He is from my country. I know him," said Efram. "What has happened?"

They watched the news broadcast in its entirety before realizing that a shooting had taken place on the island of Buyukada, and that the injured man had been airlifted to Istanbul's Central Hospital.

"We must go there," said Efram.

"Are you sure you know him?" asked Anya.

"Yes, yes, I know him. I know him well."

"Alright, we will go there tomorrow, then. Emil, may we stay with you tonight?"

"Yes, of course."

"We will sleep on the floor. That is all we will require. Tomorrow morning, we will go to the hospital."

"Thank you," said a relieved Efram. "I do not know how this will end, but I do thank you."

The vagabond couple lay quietly on the living room floor, snuggled within each other's contented arms.

"So, my sheikh," she said, "how does it feel to finally know who you are?"

"I am not completely sure of my identity just yet. But I do remember that man on the television. He is from my country;

that is all I know."

"And where is your country?"

"It is a land of beautiful horses and beautiful sunsets. Very warm, yet cool at night. The desert sands are hot and the water is very blue. And there is very much oil."

"You remember where it is, eh?"

"I remember my father and my brother. I remember I have buried them both, along with my wife. I remember certain faces, but not everyone. I remember that man on the television."

"You will remember more tomorrow, my sheikh. Tell me, what is to become of us?"

Efram did not know how to answer her. He thought for a long moment before speaking.

"What do you desire of us? Do you want to remain as friends? Or do you desire to know me more intimately?"

"I feel that meeting you is one of the most fortunate happenings of my life. I feel that you and I are meant to be together. So, to answer your question, I would very much like to know you intimately. If that is what you desire. But you are a sheikh, and I am an outlaw Gypsy."

"I feel that we have been placed along each other's path for a reason, and that Allah has brought us together. I feel very safe when I am with you. Allah must have a reason for our paths to have crossed."

"And you are very much a man directed by truth, eh?"

He smiled, leaning over to kiss her. It was their first official kiss, and though it had been a long time for both, it was, nonetheless, deep and passionate.

Chapter 37

The morning sun bathed the massive Blue and Hagia Sofia Mosques in delicate splendor, as their collective minarets stood like watchtowers guarding the ancient city with majestic honor. Anya, Efram, and Emil left for the hospital together in Emil's car. The trio were but a moment out the door when Catryna reached for the phone.

"Hello," answered Jonkur, Catryna's younger brother.

"Jonkur, you must listen to me. Do you remember Emil's sister, Anya?"

"Vaguely," answered the 34 year-old under-achieving detective, who'd been passed over for promotion the last several years.

"I know where she is."

"So what does that mean to me?" asked the slow-witted detective.

"Think about it. She has been in hiding for 20 years, and I know where she is."

"And where is that?"

"She, and a friend are going to Central Hospital. She is with that sheikh who has been on CNN, the one has been kidnapped."

"Is this true? Why would she be with him?"

"You are the detective, go find out. If you capture her, you might earn that promotion you have been waiting for."

"I deserve that promotion without having to capture a fugitive."

"I know you do. But this is an opportunity of a lifetime. Think about it. If you capture Anya and rescue that sheikh, how will that look on your record?"

She had a good point, and Jonkur knew it.

"I will go to the hospital. But why were they going there in the first place?"

"That sheikh knows somebody who was shot yesterday, in Buyukada."

Chapter 38

Callie paced the floor of her lavish hotel room like a caged lioness, trying to understand why Darkside hadn't tried to reach her. She understood his disappointment, and even his anger with her betrayal, but her confession to Inspector Edwards is what had freed the man of her dreams from prison. She was sure she'd made a favorable enough impression so that he would at least call her, not necessarily to rekindle the affair, but to check on her well-being.

Why the hell does he think I came all the way over here? She thought.

Her pride was damaged and she was hurt beyond description, but before she could talk herself out of it, decided, *if he won't come to me, I'll go to him. You son of a bitch, I hope you're worth it.*

Mixing a strong bourbon and water, she called the only person she knew besides Darkside, Sela. It was fortunate for her that she'd kept his number in her cell phone since before the cruise. Receiving no answer, she dialed the police station where Inspector Edwards had been monitoring incoming calls. Having shown her a modicum of kindness when she tried visiting Darkside in jail, she felt he might take pity and help her find the man with whom she'd fallen hopelessly in love.

"This is Inspector Edwards."

"Hello Inspector, this is this Callie Collquit, I was just calling to see if you could help me?"

"Are you calling from your hotel?"

"Why yes, I am, but..."

Interrupting her in mid-sentence, he harshly demanded, "Remain there! I am sending a car for you!"

Following a long, awkward pause he said, "I have some information about your friend. I will be there momentarily."

His tone made her blood run cold. He didn't sound like the

friendly inspector she'd spoken to the last time they were together. Sensing trouble, she grabbed her purse and ran to the taxi waiting outside the hotel entrance. The ride to the airport lasted only minutes but was long enough for her to consider her options. She knew she was in trouble with the law but didn't think it would catch up with her so quickly, on the other hand, what about Darkside? She wrestled with whether to save herself or find him.

"May I help you?" asked the ticket salesman.

"Yes, what's the next flight out of Karoumi?"

"That would be the shuttle to Dubai which is boarding now."

"I'd like a one-way please."

"Thank you and enjoy flying Dubai International."

Walking as fast as she could, she reached the plane just as the stewardess was closing the door.

Thank God, she thought. *Now, what am I going to do in Dubai?*

Inspector Edwards ordered his men to Callie's hotel.

"Yes, she's there right now," he said. "I told her I had information about her boyfriend, Prahstomank, which should hold her until you get there since he seems to be the only thing she cares about. The U.S. believes she had something to do with a man who was murdered while those two were on some cruise ship. Our job is to get her back to the states so they can deal with it. We don't need to question her. I don't even have the details, although it sounds like she had some questionable issues from her past."

The Karoumi police entered the hotel demanding Callie's room number. Finding her clothing and personals, they were confused as to whether she'd left for good or was just out somewhere. A call was made to the inspector.

"Her clothes are here, but I do not see her purse."

"Alright, if she has fled, she must have gone to the airport. Call me from there."

Callie walked through the Dubai Airport following her

short flight to the majestically, beautiful city deciding that, since they did not serve alcohol on the plane, she would have a quick drink at the bar where she could plan her next move.

"I'll have a bourbon and water, please."

She knew she had to go somewhere but couldn't decide exactly where. Turning her attention to the large television, she reached for her cigarettes when something on the screen caught her eye. It was a close-up of Darkside being airlifted to the Istanbul Hospital, the same one that Inspector Edwards had seen on the TV at police headquarters.

Oh my God, she thought. *So that's where he is.*

Gulping her drink, she rushed to the nearest ticket counter.

"When's the next flight to Istanbul?"

Seeing the look on Callie's face, the woman behind the counter quickly scanned her computer.

"In about 40 minutes."

"I'll take it. Please hurry."

With barely enough time for a second drink, she returned to the bar and ordered a double.

Having received word that Callie could not be found, and believing she'd left Karoumi to find Darkside, Inspector Edwards cunningly called off the search for the red-haired vixen. With his keen eye for character and in-depth experience with criminals from all walks of life, he'd thought there was something about her that seemed inconsistent with his mind's profile of a murderer. He felt responsible for Darkside's shooting, allowing him to escape to find his sheikh, and was now feeling guilty about Callie's safety.

Having bugged their apartments and phones since they'd reentered Karoumi, the cagey inspector knew of Darkside and Sela's plan to intercept the kidnappers and coerce them into revealing the sheikh's whereabouts. Realizing the Interpol investigators were unsuccessful in their search for the sheikh, Edwards had thought Darkside might be their best hope. Now, largely because of his willingness to allow civilians to do the job of law enforcement, an innocent man was critically injured.

I should have stopped them from their crazy scheme, he thought. *But if she's a murderer, I'm a bloody strumpet. Besides, if she finds him, they'll most likely return together. Then I'll see what she's all about.*

Chapter 39

Emil drove through the morning traffic without incident, parking the car next to the huge municipal hospital.

"We are here to see the man who was shot in Buyukada yesterday," said Efram to the young, attractive receptionist sitting behind the main lobby desk.

"He is on the fifth floor, but you will not be able to see him."

"Why is that?"

"He is in intensive care. I will check his status for you."

After calling the ICU to check Darkside's status, the receptionist turned to Efram. "I am sorry, but he remains in critical condition."

"When will we be able to see him?"

"That is up to the intensive care doctors. You may go up to the fifth floor and check in with them."

Reaching the ICU, they were told that they could go in to see Darkside one at a time, but for only five minutes. Efram followed the tall nurse clad in the blue hospital gown through the double-doors of the ICU and into a large oval-shaped room containing several beds partitioned into small, separate sections. Standing over his friend, Emil couldn't believe how helpless Darkside appeared. Fighting back tears, he tenderly clasped the injured man's lifeless hand and spoke in a very low and gentle voice.

"I am here for you, my friend. You must get well. I, I need you. We all need you."

Bowing his head in prayer, the sheikh continued, "Allah, I beseech you. Please allow this man to live. Bring him safely through this ordeal and return him to me. Return him to his countrymen."

The sheikh didn't realize it, but he was beginning to regain his memory.

"I'm sorry, sir, but your time is up," said the ICU nurse, tapping Efram on the shoulder.

Noticing the sheikh returning through the ICU doors, Emil said, "I will leave you now. I have a conference call waiting for me at home, but I will call later." Stuffing a large sum of lira into Anya's hand, he said, "Remember, my home is your home for as long as you desire." With that and a strong embrace from his sister, he walked to the elevator and was gone.

They sat together in the waiting room as Sela, who'd gone in search of a bathroom, stepped off the elevator.

"Sela," said the sheikh, as the dark-eyed man came into sight.

"My sheikh!" cried Sela, bowing before the poorly dressed monarch. Placing his hands together much like he was in prayer and bowing a second time, he said, "My sheikh, I am your loyal servant."

"Please, please," said Efram, lifting him up and hugging him. "Did you know that I have been kidnapped?"

Not knowing what to think, whether the sheikh thought that he'd had anything to do with his kidnap, Sela just nodded his head.

"This kind lady has been helping me with my return. Anya," said Efram, "come and meet Sela. He is from my country."

Anya realized from the way Sela was bowing and with the respect he was showing that Efram was indeed a royal individual.

"What is the name of your country?" asked Anya.

Efram looked to Sela for the answer.

"Tell her, Sela. Tell her of our country."

"It is called Karoumi in the United Arab Emirates. But Your Highness," asked Sela, "how did you escape the kidnappers?"

"I do not remember. I only know that I awoke at the camp

of this kind lady. Now tell me, What happened to Sasha? How is it that he has been shot?"

Sela told them about the trap that he and Darkside had set for Ramone.

"Why did you want to do that?" asked the sheikh.

"We did not know if you were alive. Sasha thought if you were still alive that he could make the kidnappers tell us where you were."

Efram's eyes moistened. Taking Sela's hand in his along with Anya's, he said softly, "I am a very, very fortunate man. I have friends like you. Bless you. Have you spoken with Sasha's doctor?" asked Efram.

Sela, somewhat embarrassed, bowed and shook his head indicating that he had not.

"I must speak with the doctor. I will return shortly." Walking back inside the ICU door, Efram ordered, "I would like to speak to the doctor."

"Are you a member of his family?" asked the nurse.

"I am his only family."

"I will place a call to the doctor for you, but I cannot guarantee anything. He is very busy."

"That is fine. I will be here all day."

Walking back to the waiting room, he paced the floor as Sela and Anya watched intently.

"So am I to call you Your Highness?" asked Anya.

Smiling at her, he didn't respond.

"Or would you like me to call you by your first name? What is your name, anyway?" she asked, attempting to lighten the moment.

Efram stopped pacing and looked at Sela. "What do they call me?" asked the sheikh.

"You are called Sheikh Efram Al-Faroud. But to me you are always Your Royal Highness," he answered proudly.

"Efram," said the sheikh. "Yes, I remember. I had a brother named Rajad. But he is dead now." He stood staring out the window until his attention was drawn toward a tall, balding man in a white coat.

"Yes, I am Doctor Stilveckish. I understand you wanted to see me?"

"Thank you, Doctor. We are friends of the man in the ICU who has been shot. His name is Sasha, and he is from Karoumi in the United Arab Emirates. What can you tell me about him?"

"He is in serious condition. The bullet passed through his kidney and his spleen, requiring extensive surgery."

"Will he live?"

"If he doesn't develop infection, but it's too early to tell. He's very serious."

"Will you please keep me informed of his progress, Doctor?"

"Of course, I think I can do that for you. You'll be able to visit him for a few minutes every hour. I'm hoping he'll regain consciousness soon. It will be good for him to see you. Also, while you're in there, talk with him. He's unconscious, but he still can hear. And he'll really want to hear from his friends."

"Thank you, Doctor. And bless you."

"You bet," said the energetic medical man.

"I am going in to visit him," said Efram, as he walked into the ICU for the third time that morning.

Anya and Sela didn't notice the three men getting off the elevator as they sat awaiting Efram's return. As the men came closer, they heard, "Anya Kozakaris?"

Anya sat without saying a word.

"Are you Anya Kozakaris?" asked the burly detective.

Realizing she'd been caught, and not wanting to bring trouble to Efram, or cause a scene in the hospital, she nodded her head.

"Anya Kozakaris, you are under arrest. You will please come with us," said Jonkur brandishing a set of handcuffs and pulling Anya's arms tightly behind her back. Sela, unable to comprehend what was happening, sat transfixed, without making a sound.

"Who is he?" ordered Jonkur.

"He is not with me," said Anya. "He is just waiting to go into the ICU."

"He is not with you?"

"No. I am alone."

The detectives escorted her over to the elevator and down to the parking garage. Not knowing what to do, Sela sat impatiently at the ICU door waiting for Efram.

Chapter 40

Callie made her way outside the Istanbul Airport to the taxi stand as the warmth of the late afternoon sun welcomed her to the Eurasian city occupying two continents.

"Central Hospital, quickly," she ordered, as the driver with the thick black moustache held open the door of the cab. Getting through the afternoon traffic was no easy task, but the elderly man had no trouble navigating the hills running parallel to the Bosporus. Callie tried not to think about the helter-skelter madness as the cab weaved dangerously through the chaotic streets. The queen of cities whizzed by like a kaleidoscope as varying aromas and stenches invaded the speeding car.

"Cen e trul Hos pee tol," said the driver in broken English as the cab came to a sudden stop in front a large complex of aged buildings. Paying the driver, Callie rushed through the lobby, seeking the whereabouts of the man she loved. Finding her way to the Intensive Care Unit, she walked up to the receptionist.

"Hello, I'm looking for Sasha Prahstomank. Is he here?" she asked.

Glancing over the list of patients, the attractive nurse responded cheerfully, "Yes, but are you a member of his family?"

"Yes, I'm his..." she stopped short, not knowing what to say. "I'm a member of his family."

"Alright, please have a seat and I will tell you when you can go in."

"Please, couldn't I see him for just a minute? I won't disturb him, I promise."

"Well, only for a moment."

"Oh, thank you. How is he, is he hurt bad?"

"He is in serious but stable condition."

Callie followed the nurse through the doors and up close to Darkside's bed. Placing her hand over her mouth, it was all she could do to hold back the tears.

"Oh God, please," she prayed. "Please, let him recover. Make him well. Please."

"Only a moment," said the nurse. "He must rest. Just wait out there with the rest of the family, and you will be able to visit every hour or so."

"The rest of the family, where?" asked Callie.

"Come, I will show you."

They walked back into the waiting room where the nurse pointed to Sela who was explaining to Efram what had happened to Anya. Upon seeing Callie, Sela's eyes widened and his face lit up, but he said not a word.

"Sela, what are you doing here?" asked a surprised Callie.

Seeing that Sela had recognized Callie, Efram immediately sensed that she was here for Darkside.

"Please, sit down. My name is Efram. How is it that you know Sasha?"

"We met several years ago in Kentucky. I, I am in love with him," sobbed Callie.

Efram looked confused saying, "I too am in love and I must now go. I must go to be with her." Turning to Sela, he asked, "Where have they taken her?"

"I do not know, Your Highness, but they all had badges, and they took her away in handcuffs."

"Then they must be policemen. I must go to her."

"Are you the sheikh?" asked Callie. "Are you the person who was kidnapped?"

"Yes. That I am."

"Oh, Your Highness, it is a blessing to finally meet you. Sasha was so worried about you. He was with me when he found out that you had been kidnapped."

"He is a fine man," said the sheikh. "But I must go now to help a friend of mine who is in trouble for helping me."

"Your Highness, may I make a suggestion?"

"Yes, of course."

"If I were you, I would find something else to wear. You don't look much like royalty in those clothes. And the Istanbul police are not going to show you much respect dressed like that."

Callie was right. Efram had been dressed in an assortment of clothing that Anya and her brother had provided, and didn't look like royalty of any kind.

"Why not check into a hotel and buy some clothes? Or better yet, have some clothing brought to you? You must maintain appearances if you are to be of any help to her."

The sheikh looked at Sela and said, "Please call Beladesh for me. Ask to speak to Najema. When you have contacted her, please inform me. And now, my dear, sit down and tell me more about you and your relationship to Sasha."

Callie told Efram the whole story about the cruise and all that had happened. Realizing that she'd fallen in love with Darkside, he could not find it in his heart to feel anything negative about her. Leaving her momentarily to speak with Najema, the sheikh ordered his private plane to leave Karoumi at once with clothing and an enormous amount of cash.

"My sheikh, we must tell the world," said a joyous Najema.

"Not yet! I have some work to do here and I do not want to be interrupted. Please, tell no one that I am here."

Chapter 41

When Efram's private plane arrived at Yesilkoy International in Istanbul, he ordered the pilot to remain with the plane on standby. Retrieving his belongings, he checked himself into the Istanbul Hilton, procuring a suite of rooms befitting his kingly stature. After showering and changing into a black suit, starched white shirt, and silver tie, he went immediately to police headquarters carrying several 100 dollar bills. Appearing regal and remembering his role of leader, he demanded...

"Do you have Anya Kozakaris incarcerated here?"

The short, heavy-set policeman in the dark green uniform stretched tightly across his protruding belly, looked at Efram asking...

"And who are you?"

Brandishing a crisp 100 dollar bill, Efram said, "I am only a friend. That is all."

The fat cop looked around insuring the coast was clear, before grabbing the money.

"She has been arrested and is in our jail. That is on the fourth floor."

"Thank you, very kindly," said the sheikh turning toward the elevator. The bills worked wonders as within minutes he was sitting directly across from Anya who'd been brought down from her cell. The couple sat on a concrete table surrounded by four stationary chairs.

Seeing the sheikh looking so royal, Anya complemented Efram saying "So, you are, indeed, a sheikh."

"I have come to get you out of here."

"It is no use, I must go on trial and then I will be taken away to prison."

"Let them try you. But I know how these political matters work. It will not be long before you will be free."

"My sheikh, you know nothing about how the Turkish Government works."

"You must trust me, I know how many governments work. This one is no different. I have power, you will see."

"What kind of power do you have in this country?"

"Power is universal. It works quite similar all over the world, especially when the power is the color of money."

Efram pulled a roll of hundreds from his pocket so that only Anya could see.

"Let us just say that I know what makes the world go around."

Looking at the large roll of bills, her eyes widened.

"Is that how you plan to get me out?"

"Do you have a better plan?"

"I, I..."

"I did not think so. I will be here until you are released. That I can promise you."

After Anya was led away, Efram went about the task of securing her release. He knew it would not be easy, but he also knew the unlimited resources he could bring to bear on the subject.

Chapter 42

Johnny Stone sat working feverishly at his word processor. He'd thought about what was happening in the Bluegrass, and he couldn't help believing that something radical was going on. It had appeared to him that the countless professionals seemed a little unsure of themselves whenever they'd offer an explanation of what was killing the foals. The latest offering was a working theory of tent caterpillar poisoning. At least that's the way he deciphered it. But some things he'd heard and read just didn't seem to add up. That's the way he saw it and that's the way he was writing it:

At present, more than 400 premature foal deaths have occurred in Central Kentucky. The equine industry, able to rule out several theoretical causes, has, to date, no definitive answer to the infamous, heart-wrenching plague.

Could it be that Mother Nature has allowed the cancerous infestation as a means of sending a wake-up call to the industry? Are we asking too much from these valuable animals which provide us so much wealth and pleasure? Are we demanding that mares bear too heavy a load by forcing them to bring forth a newborn virtually every year? Not only every year, but within the first few weeks of that year to guarantee the offspring will have a full year of development when it's classified a yearling. Could we be asking too much of the yearlings as we wean and break them, training them at such a tender age? We are pushing them harder and harder to run faster and to develop earlier so as to win those bountiful stakes races we hold so dear.

I should hope that we, who live, love, and adore these priceless animals, have more to gain from their existence than the cold, hard monetary returns of the business. I should hope that those of us who tender these animals, whether it be in assisting them in their daily endeavors, their birth, their growth, their care, and finally their death, do so through a labor of love, and with the virtuous blessings of Divine Mother herself.

Chapter 43

Jonkur's Office

Following the capture of one of Istanbul's least known criminals, Jonkur, wanting to tell his sister what he'd accomplished, hurriedly placed the call.

"Catryna, I have arrested her. She is now in jail, and I owe it all to you," said the bumbling detective.

"Did you pick up that sheikh who was with her?"

"What sheikh? I did not see a sheikh."

"The one who was kidnapped, you know the one who has been on TV?"

"I did not see a sheikh. I do not remember hearing of a sheikh."

"Jonkur, must I do everything? He was with her. They stayed at our apartment last night."

"When we went to the hospital, there was no one with her. She was alone."

"You could have been the true hero, but," Jonkur interrupted her.

"I could not have arrested this sheikh. On what charges could I have held him?"

"I did not mean for you to arrest him. You could have helped him find his way home. That is what I meant. Then you would have been on TV."

"I can never satisfy you, can I?" said the hapless detective.

"Don't, Jonkur. I am in no mood."

"Fine, then. I have your sister-in-law in custody. I guess I do owe you for that."

"Well, turn around and go back and get that sheikh. Helping him find his way home will do more for your career than anything."

"Why don't you let me be the detective here? Don't you think I know how to do my job?"

Hearing Emil's footsteps advancing toward her, she held her hand over the speaker and whispered, "I must go now."

"What is this?" shouted Emil, entering the room. Having overheard much of the conversation, he knew immediately what his treacherous wife had done.

"It is nothing. It is no concern of yours," replied the startled woman.

"You have arrested my own flesh and blood."

"I have done nothing that should not be done. She is a fugitive. And he has been kidnapped. I am not so sure that he is not a part of the plot along with Anya."

"She is my sister. How can you be so cruel?"

"She is no good. Never has been and never will be."

"That is not for you to judge. You, you are evil. You are an evil woman." With that, Emil raced to his car.

Emerging from his office, Jonkur asked his partner, "What about this sheikh? Was he kidnapped?"

"What sheikh?"

"He was with that gypsy we just brought in. We should see about him."

"Why? What is he to us?"

"What if he wasn't kidnapped? What if this is a plot?"

"A plot to what?"

"I don't know a plot to kidnap him. What if he was involved in his own kidnapping? We must check this out."

"What must we do?"

"We must go back to the hospital and find him."

"He was not there before."

"Do not argue with me. We must go!"

Chapter 44

As predicted, it didn't take long for Efram to secure Anya's release. No active record of her on file, along with the right amount of cash, was all that was necessary. Having arrived back at the hospital to be with Darkside, they were met by a frantic Emil, who'd raced from his home to warn them of Catryna's treachery.

"You have no time to waste," said Emil, excitedly. "The police along with that incompetent brother-in-law of mine will be here looking for you at any moment."

"I will not leave without Efram," said Anya.

"And I will not leave without Sasha," cried Callie.

"Yes, of course," said Efram. "We cannot leave without Sasha."

The sheikh rushed into the ICU ordering the nurse to ready Darkside for departure, claiming full responsibility. Realizing that Efram was the head-of-state of an Arabian country and not wanting to incur the wrath of his political stature, she immediately called the head nurse who placed a call to Sasha's doctor.

"We have no time for that. We must go NOW!" declared Efram. "Please, can we wheel him out of here?" It was more of an order than a question, and the nurse, understanding the gravity of the situation, yielded to their wishes.

Within minutes, the entire party, including the sheikh, Anya, Callie, Sela, and Darkside, were inside an ambulance and on their way to Istanbul's airport with lights flashing and sirens blaring. Darkside opened one eye and glared at Callie.

"How are you, honey?" she asked, stroking his forehead. He could hardly hold his head up having been placed in a wheelchair for the ride. He stared at her as his dizzy head bobbed with the sway of the ambulance.

"Sela," ordered the sheikh, "please call to ready the

plane."

Sela immediately phoned the pilot who'd remained on standby after having delivered the sheikh's clothes and money. The entourage made its way through the busy streets as Jonkur and his partner entered the hospital only to find they were a step behind.

"Where did they go?" ordered the burly detective.

"To the airport."

"How long have they been gone?"

"About five minutes. But I am not sure," answered the nurse.

"Alright, call this in," ordered Jonkur.

"And what will I say?" asked his partner.

"Just tell them to put out a bulletin and stop that ambulance."

"Can we stop an ambulance?"

"Just call it in," he ordered as they ran for their car.

The ambulance made the trip in record time, pulling aside the belly of the plane. Sela and Efram carried Darkside up the stairway placing him across the rear seats.

"Just lay here, my friend. We will have you home as soon as possible," said Efram.

Slamming the door, Efram ordered the pilot to take off. But as he looked toward the open door of the cockpit, a different face appeared from behind the bulkhead.

"So," said the strange voice, "we meet again, eh Sela?"

"Ramone!" cried Sela. "What are you do..." he stopped short, peering down the barrel of a pistol.

"Who are you?" ordered the sheikh.

"Let us just say that I am an old friend. And I am here to collect on an old debt."

"So it was YOU who ordered my kidnapping?"

"And you," said Ramone pointing his gun at Darkside. "You tricked me. But I showed you. How does that bullet hole feel?"

Having grasped the situation in his foggy brain, Darkside

pulled himself partially upright. "Did you really think you could just kidnap my sheikh and get away with it?" he gasped in a feeble voice.

"You are in no condition to stop me now," said Ramone. "Now, I will finish what I started out to do."

Seeing he was about to fire, Callie shouted "NO!" before diving in front of Darkside to protect him. The first bullet ripped through her blouse, creasing the top of her shoulder, while the second bullet missed her entirely, lodging in the seat beside Darkside's head. But the third bullet fired stopped the merciless terrorist in his tracks.

Reeling about with a stunned look on his face, his eyes open wide and his mouth agape, Ramone gazed at Sela as his knees buckled. Unable to see that Sela had pulled his 9mm from beneath his shirt, Ramone dropped his gun and fell, reeling in pain. The big man looked down at the blood gushing from his shoulder before falling to the cabin floor, unconscious.

Efram ran to the cockpit to see about the pilot. Bound and gagged, the hapless man sat wide-eyed behind the controls.

"Oh, thank Allah, you are not harmed," said Efram, untying the pilot's hands and gag. "Now, we must hurry; we are being chased."

"This is UAEK zero one, requesting permission to start engines and taxi," barked the pilot, following Efram's instructions.

"Go ahead, UAEK zero one. You are cleared to start your engines."

"What are we to do with him?" asked Sela nodding toward Ramone.

"Open the door and place him on the ground," ordered the sheikh. "We have no time to deal with him."

As the plane received clearance to taxi, Efram could see the detectives' car speeding toward them, the blue lights flashing.

"UAEK zero one, this is central. We have been ordered by

the police to detain your aircraft. Please hold and stop your engines."

"Ignore that," ordered the sheikh, who'd taken over the co-pilot's seat. "We must go NOW!"

The sheikh and the pilot pushed the throttles forward as the tiny plane lurched onto the runway just ahead of the chasing detectives. Realizing they would be queued for takeoff behind several other airplanes, the pilot turned onto a shorter runway and, without clearance, pushed the little plane crosswise into the departing traffic.

"Well, here goes," he said forcing the throttles forward to maximum power.

Seeing that the plane was about to take off, Jonkur ordered his partner to shoot the tires.

"Can we shoot tires of a moving plane?"

"Of course we can; they're getting away."

"But they have not broken any law," responded the hapless detective, as Jonkur sped along beside the plane.

"Just shoot the tires."

"You shoot the tires."

As the detectives argued, the little plane lifted off into the backwash of a departing L-1011.

"Look out," screamed Jonkur, as the giant plane roared less than 10 feet over their heads. Swerving to avoid the plane, the detectives found themselves heading directly into the oncoming traffic.

The sheikh's plane nearly flipped over passing through the vortex of spiraling air, but the pilot, using every ounce of strength, gained control as the right-side wing came within inches of the ground.

"Now that's what I call close," said the pilot. Efram, with his eyes closed, prayed, "Thank you, Allah."

Bringing the car to a screeching stop alongside the runway, the detectives ran to the nearby grass like two frightened children.

Chapter 45

They made the trip in less than 14 hours, driving through the night down I-75. Once in Florida, Gwen submitted her resignation before packing her furniture into the large truck she'd rented for the return trip, having decided to stay with Dr. Pehlagrem temporarily while looking for her own place. Tuck had offered to keep her things in one of the barns at Fairhaven until she found one.

They weren't home more than two days when Tuck called to invite her to go on a drive with him. It was Sunday, and the air was sweet and unseasonably clear.

"Hey," said Tuck, "I'll pick you up at Doctor P's in half an hour."

"Great! And don't be late."

They drove to Fairhaven where Tuck had taken an old, unused road back to a remote pasture. Divided by a winding creek which ran down through the center of the farm, it was shaded by several weeping willow trees.

"Wow! I've never seen anything as pretty as this."

"This is my special place. Whenever I want to just get away from it all, this is where I come."

Walking over to the creek, they gazed at the sparkling water flowing past an old mill-house.

"That's old Tom's Mill. That must be over a hundred years old," said Tuck.

"Where's the paddle wheel?"

"Oh that's been gone since I can't remember. Guess they didn't want anyone getting hurt on it. You know how kids are."

"Yeah, and I'm looking at one right now."

"Ha. You got that right. If that wheel'd been on there when I was younger, I probably wouldn't be here right now."

Gwen sat down next to the creek removing her sandals, and placing her feet in the streaming water.

"Wow! That's coooold."

"Yeah, that water never really warms up. Just dries up. But as long as it's flowing, it's good and cold."

Tuck walked behind her and pulled a small rounded box from his shirt pocket. Sitting down beside her, he placed it in her lap. Not noticing immediately, she sat back on her hands looking downstream toward the old mill. The sunlight reflected beautifully through the half-carat diamond as Gwen looked down.

"Oh, my God," she said. "Oh, my God, is this for me?"

"Well, it ain't for me."

She quickly placed the ring on her finger and held it up to the light.

"Tuck, I don't know what to say. I, I'm."

"Will you marry me, Gwen?"

Turning to face him with tears in her eyes and a smile pulling at the ends of her lips, the brilliant microbiologist nodded her head and whispered the words he so longed to hear,

"Yes, Tucker Flannery, I will marry you."

They remained side by side, his arm around her shoulder for several long moments as the warm breeze wafted though the willow trees until Tuck said, "Come on, I want to show you something."

They drove over to a large field where the yearlings were stabled. Squinting through the sunlight Tuck pointed to a large chestnut with two white feet and a triangular star on his head.

"That's Jewel Thief's colt," said Tuck. "Isn't he beautiful?"

"He sure is. I haven't noticed him before."

"I'm not going to get my hopes up, but I've got big plans for him. He looks sound and his daddy's huge."

"What about his momma?"

"Oh, she's over in the other pasture. She was one of the mares whose foal was stillborn this year, Sugar Berry."

"What a shame."

"Yeah, well so far we've been pretty lucky. We've only

lost four. Hell, there are some farms that have been devastated."

"So what are you going to name him?"

"Don't know, any ideas?"

"Why not, Sugar Thief?"

"That's not bad, Gwen. I like it. Okay, Sugar Thief, you've got your momma and daddy's blood as well as their names. I sure hope you can run."

"Run," said Gwen, "he'll fly."

Chapter 46

Karoumi

The tattered and weary entourage made its way back to Karoumi, as was met by a band of reporters, detectives, policemen, and crowds of well-wishers. The small country went into an immediate state of celebration as the people came to realize their beloved sheikh was home safe and sound.

Darkside had been taken to the Karoumi Hospital where, after several days of rest, was strong enough to receive a visit from Inspector Edwards.

"I should be mad at you, Mr. Prahstomank. But under the circumstances, I believe I can live with it."

"I had to do what I did. You would do the same, if it were a member of your family."

"Yes, of course. By the way, did you know that woman you were with? Did you know she is under suspicion for murder?"

Not believing what he'd heard, Darkside just shook his head.

"She had met up with one of her former prostitute friends aboard the ship upon which you were travelling. This friend of hers and some others managed to throw a ruthless gangster overboard while you were all out to sea. You wouldn't happen to know anything about that, would you?"

"NO certainly not!"

"No, of course you wouldn't. But I think she does. Tell me, how well did you know this woman before you went on the cruise with her?"

"I hardly knew her at all. I was very attracted to her, but I hardly knew her. I had met her a few years before at a Derby party."

The inspector stood for a long moment before asking, "I don't suppose you know her whereabouts?"

"I do not. I have not seen her."

"She wasn't on that plane with you and the sheikh on your return from Istanbul?"

"I have no idea. I was quite unconscious."

"Very well, then. If you do run across her, please let me know."

Darkside nodded. Under heavy medication, he hadn't thought about Callie or anything else for several days and was burdened by the mention of her being involved with murder. He didn't have to think about her for very long; it was time for his medicine and another painless nap.

Chapter 47

With all the celebration of the sheikh's return, and the need for Efram to be everywhere at once, Anya was left in the hands of Najema for the first several days. Not wanting to bother the sheikh and feeling rather out of place with all the ornate surroundings, she felt that the best thing for her was to return to her country and her people.

"I should really begin my journey home," she told Najema early one morning, packing her meager belongings.

"Why must you go? Do you not feel welcome here?"

"It is not that. I know I am welcome, but I am not from here. I do not fit this lifestyle. I will be a burden. No, I must return, quickly before your sheikh knows that I am gone."

"I do not think you should go without my sheikh's knowledge. He would be very upset if you were not here and he was not aware that you had gone. I believe he is quite fond of you."

"But what could I ever be to him? I am just a Gypsy, and he is a king."

"Kings need love too," said Najema.

"I know that I have developed feelings for him. But I am not so sure about his feelings. If I stay and he is not interested in me, then I will become a burden. And that I do not want."

"Well, do you not think he has the same feelings as you?"

"I am afraid to take the chance. What if he does not? Then what will I do?"

"What do you want? Do you want him to love you? If you do, then going away now will hurt your chances for that."

"Can you see me as his queen? As any queen, for that matter?" asked Anya.

"You were the one who saved my sheikh. You protected

him, fed and clothed him, and guided him back to his home. Yes, I can definitely see you as my queen, and my countrymen will feel the same."

Anya felt tears as she sat next to Najema. Taking her hand, she said softly, "That is the kindest thing anyone has ever said to me. Thank you."

They sat together for a few moments before Najema broke the silence. "Now, I must take you shopping. If you are going to be a queen, you must start looking like a queen."

"Are you sure, Najema? Are you sure I could be a queen?"

"Not a word more about it. Come on, the day is young and we have much to do. The next time you see him, you will look like the Queen of Karoumi."

For the next several hours, they bought Anya a complete ensemble of shoes, robes, dresses, suits, hats, gloves and lingerie. Then it was off to the hairdresser where she had her hair tinted, removing the yellow and gray and her nails done. She looked every bit the part of regalia standing in front of the mirror in her suite.

"Now," asked Najema, "do you feel like a queen?"

Anya could not speak. She never knew how beautiful she was, and now she could see how stunning she looked in the new clothes.

"What do you think he will say?"

"I don't think he will be able to say anything. I think that he will be without words."

"When am I supposed to see him again?"

"You will dine with him this evening, in about an hour. Just time enough for a bath and some primping."

"Primping? What is primping?"

"That is what every woman does. It is our rite of passage, and especially when one has dinner with a king."

Chapter 48

It was late as Darkside dressed quietly and slipped out of the hospital room into the secrecy of night. Arriving at Sela's apartment without notice and heavily medicated, he asked, "Is she here?"

As Sela opened the door, Darkside could see Callie sitting inside.

"Oh, Sasha," she cried moving to embrace her former lover, even though her arm was in a sling due to the bullet she'd taken in her shoulder.

"Remain away," he demanded, moving painfully into the apartment. "You are a criminal. They are looking for you regarding your friend you met on the ship. They believe you had something to do with a murder."

"Sasha," she pleaded. "I can assure you, I had nothing..."

"It is no business of mine what you have done. I have arranged a plane to fly you home tonight. From there, you will be on your own. That is all I can do for you."

Grimacing in pain, he walked toward the door. Looking back at her, he tried to smile, but found that he could not. Looking at Sela and then back at Callie and then down at the floor for an extended moment, he finally said...

"I had the best time of my life while I was with you. A time which I will never forget, and for that I am grateful." His voice was breaking and on the verge of tears as he said, "Good luck to you, Callie. I...," and with that, he was gone.

"So," said Callie, "I guess that's that."

Looking at Sela, she asked, "I don't suppose you could take me to this plane he's arranged for me, do you?"

Callie nursed her broken heart and sore shoulder over the Atlantic with the bourbon she'd brought with her. She knew she'd met the man of her dreams, but, for once, a man had resisted her. She knew she'd made an impression on him and planted the seeds for a loving future. Now she just had to make a plan. She'd never been a woman to quit when the going got tough, especially when she wanted something or someone as badly as she wanted Darkside. She had a lot of moxie and, in her mind, things weren't over yet.

Hell, baby, she thought, *this is only the beginning.*

Chapter 49

Efram had planned to address the nation through the local media, but when CNN heard of the plan, they wanted to film his speech for re-broadcast.

It was a night to remember as the sheikh spoke to his countrymen. Shortly before the momentous occasion, he'd awarded Sela the Golden Scepter, Karoumi's highest medal for bravery. Facing the microphones, Efram began his speech as the citizens of Karoumi gathered around televisions and radios to listen to their charismatic leader. He started with a prayer.

"Allow us, my fellow countrymen, to offer our thanks for what has transpired. One of our more challenging events has become one of the most gracious moments in the history of our country. I thank each of you for your prayers, your loyalty, your love, and most of all for the fact that we are a family."

Winking at Anya, he concluded, "A family united under the greatest protection of all, the protection of Allah."

I was never known how many dollars it took to secure Anya's release, and that's just the way Efram wanted it. She was a known criminal who had escaped detection for over two decades, and was considered a menace to the Turkish people, so he price, whatever it was, did not come cheap. Needless to say, Efram thought that no matter the price, he had come away with a real bargain.

And as the sun set over the white sands surrounding the smallest Trucial State of the United Arab Emirates, the people of Karoumi settled into the night with the knowledge that their country and their leader, was once, again safe in his own bed, and all was well.

Chapter 50

Darkside moved slowly and with the help of a cane, but there was only one place he wanted to be. He stood at the fence overlooking a herd of yearlings chasing each other carelessly through the grassy pasture. Although his mind was on the horses, his heart was elsewhere. He'd been bitten by the ruthless parasite of love, had lost the battle and was now drowning in the backwash of its flight.

Workers scurried around him as did the yearlings, but his thoughts were far away, tethered to a strikingly beautiful red-haired lady who spoke softly and with a southern accent. He could almost smell her gentle perfume wafting in the air as he seemed to find her reflection everyplace he looked.

Was I right? he thought. *Should I have sent her away? How many others would have taken a bullet for me?*

His daydream was interrupted by..."Look at that black colt," said a stable-hand from inside the fence. "He looks regal, does he not?"

Darkside nodded allowing his focus to drift over to the gangly black colt prancing outside the herd.

"He walks like a king," said the stable-hand.

A king, thought Darkside, *Karoumi King*.

As the sun reached for the desert's edge, announcing the close of another day in Paradise, his thoughts rang with Callie's questions as he could hear her voice cracking...

"Haven't you ever done anything that you've regretted? Haven't you ever wanted to undo something, but couldn't? Haven't you ever been ashamed of yourself?"

He knew he had, and now he'd wished he'd told her about the nose spray and the dead foals he'd caused and how he'd actually arranged for a man's murder. He wished he'd told her so many things, but that was all over now.

But, he thought, *at least I was able to get her out of the country. Out of harm's way.*

He knew that he helped to avoid her almost certain arrest. His past was littered with so many dark days and he was on the dark side of those days. And, he was going to have to live with himself no matter what.

But regardless how he measured it, it was just him and his conscience, him, his conscience, and Allah.

Acknowledgments

I would like to express my appreciation to the following individuals who have blessed this work with their participation:

My wife, Judy, my first-line editor and constant companion.

Sharon Bradley for her beautiful cover design.

Joni Stowe for her expertise in the art of writing and editing.

Professor Jan Holland for her righteous knowledge of the English language.

Royal Caribbean's Monarch of the Seas for providing me the most enjoyable vacation I have ever had.

Other books by Robert Monahan:

- The Thoroughbred Conspiracy
- Unbridled Terror
- Coal Dust

Visit my website: **www.robertmonahan.net**